Praise for *Tru & Nelle*

"*Tru and Nelle* is a gloriously realized return to the world of *To Kill a Mockingbird*. Neri's fictional take on the childhood friendship of Lee and Capote is both funny and deeply poignant—an utterly charming mystery-adventure that is part *Huck Finn*, part *Anne of Green Gables*, and part *Scooby Doo*. It just might become a timeless classic itself."—Margaret Stohl, #1 *New York Times* bestselling coauthor of the Beautiful Creatures series

★ "Charming and elegantly written . . . an engaging portrait of two children's world before they became famous."
—*Kirkus Reviews*, starred review

★ "In a bold but rewarding gambit, Neri imagines the childhood friendship of Harper Lee and Truman Capote—yet still making it entirely his own."—*Booklist*, starred review

★ "In his terrific, often very funny middle-grade novel *Tru and Nelle*, Coretta Scott King Honor author G. Neri (*Yummy*) reimagines this heartwarming, close-knit friendship in a small Southern community that drips with heat and Spanish moss."
—*Shelf Awareness*, starred review

"If you've ever wanted to run through the backyards of dusty old Maycomb, Alabama, in search of high adventure and mystery, just like Scout, Dill, and Jem, then this is your chance. I hope you're up for some fun!"—Charles J. Shields, author of *Mockingbird: A Portrait of Harper Lee*

"Wonderfully imaginative . . . affirms the mysterious and glorious ways that friendship reaches across boundaries of all sorts to claim unexpected kinship." — Gary D. Schmidt, author of Newbery Honor books *Lizzie Bright and the Buckminster Boy* and *The Wednesday Wars*

"[*Tru and Nelle*] reads like a classic. Middle-grade readers will be touched by their resilience in the face of dark family and societal situations." — *San Francisco Book Review*

"A delightful tale. . . . *Tru and Nelle* will enchant younger readers." — BookPage

"There is a gentle, azalea-scented goodness to *Tru and Nelle* that young readers may fall for, and which grants space to the racial ugliness of the past without dwelling exclusively on it." — *USA Today*

"A love letter to two cultural icons. . . . Neri's homage envisions a deep, rewarding relationship between two children before the literary world knew their names." — *Horn Book*

"I think it's a valuable read for your kid, especially in today's climate. . . . It's also a funny, sweet, and heartbreaking read wrapped in a detective story. This is a good one that works on a lot of levels. Read it with your kids." — Michael Buckley, author of *The Sisters Grimm* and *N.E.R.D.S.*

"Heartwarming, funny, and beautifully crafted; readers will be sucked in from the very first chapter." — *School Library Journal*

Tru & Nelle
A Christmas Tale

Tru & Nelle

A Christmas Tale

a novel by G. Neri

HOUGHTON MIFFLIN HARCOURT
Boston   New York

www.hmhco.com

The text was set in Adobe Caslon Pro.

Library of Congress Cataloging-in-Publication Data
Names: Neri, Greg, author.
Title: Tru & Nelle : a Christmas tale / by G. Neri.
Other titles: Tru and Nelle, a Christmas tale
Description: Boston ; New York : Houghton Mifflin Harcourt, [2018]. |
Summary: Two years after choosing his mother in a Christmas-season
custody hearing, Truman Capote runs away to spend Christmas in
Monroeville, Alabama, with best friend, Nelle Harper Lee,
who gives him courage to stay true to himself.
Identifiers: LCCN 2017002392 |
ISBN 9781328685988 (hardback) | ISBN 9781328829009 (ebook)
Subjects: LCSH: Capote, Truman, 1924–1984—
Juvenile fiction. | Lee, Harper—Juvenile fiction. | CYAC: Capote, Truman,
1924–1984—Fiction. | Lee, Harper—Fiction. | Friendship—Fiction. |
Christmas—Fiction. | Trials—Fiction. |
Mystery and detective stories. | Monroeville (Ala.)—History—
20th century—Fiction. | BISAC: JUVENILE FICTION / Social Issues /
Friendship. | JUVENILE FICTION / Holidays & Celebrations / Christmas
& Advent. | JUVENILE FICTION / Historical / United States /
20th Century. | JUVENILE FICTION / Books & Libraries. |
JUVENILE FICTION / Mysteries & Detective Stories. | JUVENILE
FICTION / Family / Stepfamilies. Classification: LCC PZ7.N4377478
To 2018 | DDC [Fic]—dc23
LC record available at https://lccn.loc.gov/2017002392

Manufactured in the United States of America
DOC 10 9 8 7 6 5 4 3 2 1
4500675128

For Maggie and Zola,
as always

I don't care what anybody says about me as long as it isn't true.

—Truman Capote

Ten Days Before Christmas, 1935

1
Surprise Visit

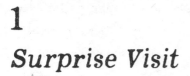

"D o you think he'll be any taller?" asked Big Boy.

Nelle squinted into the hot Alabama sun. It was a balmy seventy-eight degrees in December. So much for a white Christmas. They'd been standing on the side of the red dirt road from Montgomery for more than an hour. The only sign of life was the buzzards circling overhead.

"Nah. I reckon he'll still be a shrimp," she answered.

Big Boy took off his glasses and wiped the dust from them with his shirtsleeve. "Maybe he'll be all fancy and big-city now," he said absent-mindedly.

Nelle looked at him like he was crazy. "You remember that white suit he used to wear all the time? I think he was the only boy in Monroeville who even *had* a suit!"

Nelle was the kind of ten-year-old girl who wouldn't be caught dead in a dress. She wore her usual tomboy outfit: beat-up overalls and white T-shirt, with bare feet. "Heck, he couldn't be more highfalutin and big-city if he tried," she added, spitting into the dirt and watching it turn burgundy.

Big Boy was a farmer's boy; no matter how many baths he took, he always smelled like cows, something the girls never let him forget. Despite his nickname, he was not overly big for an eleven-year-old.

A red cloud rising from the horizon caught his eye.

They stood and stared at the gathering cloud as it grew closer. It took a few seconds before they could see a black speck causing the red tornado of dust. A minute later, the black speck became a fancy black convertible.

"Finally," said Big Boy.

The closer it came, the faster Nelle's heart seemed to beat. It had been over two years since their best friend, Truman, had been ripped from their lives. In the beginning, it seemed like she'd gotten a letter from him at least once a week—stories about high-society life in New York, the endless parties, sightings of famous writers and actors, and skyscrapers tall enough to touch the sun.

Then, as winter gave way to spring, and another fall and winter passed, the stories grew shorter and shorter, until they tapered off altogether. She had not heard a peep from him for the past five months—that is, until his older cousin Jenny received a telegram saying he, his mother, and stepdad were suddenly coming to town for the holidays.

"Maybe we should call him Sherlock. You know, for old times' sake?" asked Big Boy.

Nelle broke into a smile, but it quickly faded. Truman was eleven and had been going to some expensive private school. He was sure to be different. Maybe he wouldn't even remember them. Maybe he'd forgotten all the adventures they'd shared or even the mysteries they'd solved together.

The car came up on them fast. At the wheel was a dark-skinned man in a fancy tan suit, smoking a fat cigar. A woman was asleep in the passenger seat.

"Is that them?" asked Big Boy, excited.

A horn blasted, sending Nelle and Big Boy scrambling to the side of the road. As the car flew past, Nelle caught a glimpse of someone in the back seat, slumped out of sight, his white-blond hair blowing in the wind.

They were swallowed up in a tailwind of dust. "Come on." Nelle spat as they grabbed their bikes and followed in the car's wake.

The automobile eluded them, but Monroeville was just a dusty old hamlet and not so big that they couldn't spot a fancy car like that. As Nelle and Big Boy rode through the town square, shopkeepers were just putting up their Christmas decorations, which was always a funny sight, given that a Monroeville Christmas was never like the snowy ones in the picture shows. A winter heat wave was not uncommon in these parts.

"Maybe we should stop and get a Christmas present for him?" suggested Big Boy.

"First we need to find out why he's really here. Something smells fishy to me," said Nelle.

In front of the hardware store, Nelle spotted Mr. Barnett, who had a wooden leg, holding a plastic snowman and staring off down the road. She followed his gaze right to the fancy car, which was parked smack-dab in front of A.C. Lee's office!

Nelle and Big Boy ditched their bikes by one of the grand oak trees that ran down the center of Alabama Avenue. They made their way through a small group of gawkers surrounding the convertible. Truman was not in the back seat. But somebody had filled in the *New York Times* crossword puzzle with the scribbled scrawl of a child.

Nelle gazed up at the second-floor window of her father's office. "Do you think . . . ?"

Big Boy shrugged. There was only one way to find out.

They tore up the stairs as quietly as they could, pausing in front of the second-floor office door on which was etched these words:

Amasa Coleman Lee

Lawyer   Legislator

Financial Manager   Editor at Large

Instead of knocking, Nelle motioned Big Boy toward an unmarked side door, which led to a storage room filled with boxes and cleaning supplies.

"What are we doing here?" whispered Big Boy.

She shushed him and closed the door behind them. They stood in the dark except for a crack of light that emanated from another door in the back of the room.

Nelle headed for the light. "That's A.C.'s office," she whispered.

They tiptoed forward until a voice stopped them dead in their tracks.

"*Who does he think he is?*" shouted a woman. "To do this around the holidays? That is so typical of him. Ruining it for everyone!"

Nelle looked at Big Boy. That was Truman's mother, Lillie Mae, talking.

"Nina, Nina, don't let him upset you so," said a thickly accented male voice.

"Nina?" whispered Big Boy. Nelle shushed him again so she could hear.

"*Mi corazón*. He cannot win, he cannot," said the man. "Isn't that right, Mr. A.C.?"

"Is that Tru's dad—I mean, stepdad . . . What's his name? Cuban Joe?" asked Big Boy. "And who's *he* talking about?"

There was a pause. Nelle could hear a light tapping; A.C. always tapped a small pocketknife against a table whenever he was thinking.

Her father spoke slowly and deliberately. "Nothing is ever certain in this world. But a wounded and cornered animal should never be underestimated."

"Then we should do what you do to a rabid dog," hissed Nina. "You put him out of his misery!"

"Nina, *mi amor!*" cried Joe. "I sympathize with your ex-husband. He is wounded because he lost the battle for your heart. Don't you see that all he can do is to try to get back at you? *Óyeme,* listen to me: desperate men do desperate things. His only resort is to take our Truman away from us."

Nelle took a step back and bumped into a box that had an old lamp sitting on top of it. She turned just in time to see the lamp teeter on the edge, and before she could grab it—

Crash!

"What was that?" said Joe.

There was the creak of a chair, the sound of footsteps on the wooden floor, and the rattling of the door handle. Nelle and Big Boy stood frozen like deer in headlights.

The door swung open and the silhouette of A.C. Lee towered over them. "Seems like word has gotten out. Nelle, Big Boy, why don't you join us instead of spying on Mr. and Mrs. Capote from the broom closet."

Nelle's eyes fell on Lillie Mae, who was dressed like a Nina, or what Nelle imagined someone named Nina might look like. She had a sleek bob of a haircut, long lashes, and a shiny dress Nelle thought a woman might wear to a dinner club. Holding her hand was Joe, dark-skinned and built like a boxer, with a barrel chest, but his horn-rim glasses made him look soft and kind.

A.C. cleared his throat. Nelle gave him her saddest puppy-dog-eyed look. "We didn't mean nothing by it, A.C., honest. We didn't mean to spy. We was just curi—"

Her eyes fell on Truman, who was sitting in a chair in the corner, scribbling in a small notebook. He looked up at her. His eyes were just as pale blue as she remembered. He seemed older but somehow smaller than before, his feet not even touching the floor. His blond hair was longer and whiter, if that was possible, and he was dressed in a simple suit with tennis shoes.

"Hiya—" she started to say.

Lillie Mae cut her off. "Great! Now *everyone* is going to know," she said, rising from her seat. "These two cannot be trusted."

"But—" said Big Boy.

"Nina, they are just children looking for their friend," said Joe. "They won't say a word. The custody hearing will be but a simple matter that no one needs to know about. Right, kids?"

"Yes, sir," they both answered while staring at Truman.

Nelle had to ask: "Does that mean you're going to live with your dad—with Arch Persons?"

Before Truman could answer, Lillie Mae growled through her dark red lipstick, "If I hear that you two have been gossiping—"

A.C. cut in and ushered Nelle and Big Boy toward the office

door. "Perhaps it's best if you go. You can catch up with Truman back at the house," he said.

"But . . . Tru—" Nelle said, looking over her shoulder. Truman just watched as A.C. gently pushed them into the hallway.

"And not a word to anyone," said A.C. before closing the door in their faces.

Nelle and Big Boy looked at each other.

"Boy, she is the most uptight person I ever met," said Nelle.

"Why does he call her Nina?" said Big Boy. "Did you see the way they dressed? All high-society and the like. Joe must be loaded."

Nelle snapped her fingers. "Maybe Arch is trying to kidnap Truman for ransom. I hear he's lost everything," she said.

"I can still hear you," said A.C. on the other side of the door. "Go home. *Now*."

Nelle sighed as she and Big Boy turned and headed slowly out into the sunlight.

On the way home, they paused in front of Cousin Jenny's house. Nelle could see that preparations had been under way all morning in anticipation of Truman's return. They'd broken out the Christmas decorations earlier than usual, since they knew Truman loved the holidays. Nelle could smell the delectable scent of Sook's lemon meringue pie, Tru's favorite, coming from the kitchen. But she and Big Boy needed to talk about what they'd heard back at A.C.'s. And there was only one place for secret discussions: the treehouse.

Since Truman left, the treehouse in the double chinaberry tree that divided their properties had not seen much use. Big Boy lived on a farm out on Drewry Road, and without Truman around, he rarely came over to see Nelle, who was clearly becoming a young woman, despite her best efforts not to.

They snuck past Jenny's house and made their way up the ladder, Big Boy first. When he poked his head up through the escape hatch, he stopped in his tracks.

"Hey, Big Boy. Take your sweet time, why don'tcha?" said Nelle. "I can't hang around here all day, you know."

"Um . . ."

Nelle saw Big Boy glance down at her nervously.

She stiffened. "Is it a snake?"

When Arch Persons's head came into view, she saw that she was partially right.

"What're *you* doing here?" she said. "Can't you read?" She pointed to the No Adults Allowed sign posted by the entrance.

"*Ho, ho, ho!* Good to see you too," Arch said. "Now get your behinds up here before anyone spots you." Big Boy squeezed by him and Arch extended his hand to Nelle.

"I can make my own way, thank you very much," she growled.

When she came up into the fort, Arch was peering at Jenny's house through a cutout window. "They're still at A.C.'s office," said Big Boy.

"So you know, then," said Arch, as if some big secret had been revealed. He looked silly, a large man in an old suit and cheap glasses scrunched up in a kids' treehouse.

"You hiding from the law again?" said Nelle, suspicious. "I thought you were headed to prison."

"Those charges were all hat and no cattle, for Pete's sake," said Arch. "I'm a churchgoing man now, I'll have you know."

"Uh-huh . . ." Nelle wasn't buying it. "Look, we don't know nothing and ain't interested in any scheme you got cooking up in that head o' yours."

Big Boy cleared his throat. "Well, except that Nina was all upset that you was trying to take Truman from her and all—"

Arch beamed. "Really? You heard that? Serves 'Nina' right."

Nelle stared daggers at Big Boy.

"Just calm down, honey. I'm here to give you an early Christmas present, so give the theatrics a rest, will ya?" Arch said, trying to find a comfortable position to squat in. "You *do* want Truman back, don'tcha?"

Big Boy glanced at Nelle, who tried to contain herself. "What do you mean?" she asked cautiously.

Arch knew he'd gotten her attention. "I mean, if Truman plays his cards right, he could be back to live at his cousin Jenny's by the end of the week, and I mean for *good*."

Nelle stared at him closely. She knew better than to trust Arch Persons. There was no scheme he didn't like as long as there was something in it for him. "What's he gotta do?"

He sighed, as if it pained him to say. "Look, you both know

as well as I do that his mother doesn't really care for him. She's a treacherous woman who's just using Truman as a pawn to get back at me," said Arch. "Well, I'm sick and tired of that boy getting used. I'm not trying to get custody. She's got me on that count. But if I win, I might be able to—" He paused, looked around dramatically, then whispered, "Look, I've been talking to the judge, and he agrees that living at Jenny's, surrounded by his elder cousins, would be best for the boy. So if I win, I'd do what's best for him."

"You mean . . . you'd have him move back here forever?" asked Big Boy.

Arch nodded. "If I can put Truman on the stand at the hearing tomorrow and he gets going about the fast life they all live up there in New York, with all the parties, gambling, and drinking and who knows what else—any judge in his right mind would see Lillie Mae for what she is: a sinner who married a gambling, dark-skinned foreigner for his money, for Pete's sake. She's an irresponsible child who needs to be stopped."

Big Boy's mind was racing. "So what do you want *us* to do?" he asked.

Arch smiled softly. "Talk to Truman. Get him to see that what they're promising him ain't on the level, that he'd be much better off here with Sook and Queenie and you two mutts."

"What's she promising him?" asked Nelle. But a car started honking and they all peered out the window just in time to see Joe pulling up to Jenny's house.

"Good, they're here," said Arch. "Look at 'em. Their money

offends me. People are suffering in this town and they act like it's still the Roaring Twenties. They've got plenty of dough, but they come after *me* for child support? It ain't right." Nelle could see his face turning red.

His voice dropped and got real serious. "Now get down there and start asking him about all the scandalous things they do up there in the big city. I know how Truman loves spicing up stories to entertain folks. That's all he's gotta do. Perform for a crowd. Sell it like he's being brought up in an immoral way."

"Is he?" asked Nelle.

Arch leaned forward. "They don't call it the Big Apple for nothing. It's the place of the original sin. I heard those two have dealings with gangsters and all kinds of nefarious people. Believe me, the big city is no place to raise a boy as delicate as Truman."

Nelle and Big Boy watched the greetings play out from behind a bush. Truman's older cousins — Jenny, who was the matriarch, and Bud, the so-called man of the house — came out onto the front porch. Jenny was always dressed like she meant business, prim and proper but tough as a bantam rooster. Bud was just the opposite — tall and thin with a mountain of white hair, he always looked like he'd just woken up from a nap.

Bud's face lit up when he saw Joe and Lillie Mae getting out of the car. But Jenny's mouth turned into a scowl. She and Lillie Mae always butted heads, and her showing up on such short notice was never a good sign.

"Jeenneeee — so beeeauuuutiful!" said Joe, bounding up the

12

stairs and trapping Jenny in a hug. She managed to squirm out of his arms and pushed him into Bud. "And, Bud, looking gooood! Come, Nina, it's a Christmas reunion! Even though there's no snow!"

"It never snows here. Why, the children don't even know how to ice-skate," said Nina.

Jenny stared at her. "Hello, *Lillie Mae.*"

She gritted her teeth. "It's Nina. People in New York use more sophisticated names."

"Oh, *please,*" said Jenny. "You were born Lillie Mae and you'll die Lillie Mae, regardless of what you call yourself. You can't escape your past. Now, where is that child of yours?" she said, looking at the car.

Truman was sitting in the back seat, reading the newspaper.

"Why's Tru acting so weird?" whispered Big Boy. "You'd think he'd be excited to be back."

"I don't know," said Nelle. "But he sure does look full of himself."

"Little Chappie!" shouted Bud. "Get yourself up here so we can have a look-see!"

Truman put down his paper and straightened his tie. He calmly got out of the car and walked over to them like a little aristocrat.

He approached the stairs as if he were being introduced to a new group of adults for the first time. He held his hand out to Bud, who looked at him quizzically. Bud grinned, revealing a mouthful of yellow teeth, pushed the hand away, and gave him a big ol' hug. "How's my little writer doing? When you gonna write a story about me?"

"Let me see him!" said Jenny. She put her hand on the side of Tru's face and then suddenly leaned down and bear-hugged him too. But she felt awkward and let go, smoothing out his hair.

"My, look at you," she said, patting him on the head. "Getting bigger, I see."

"I'm the tallest one in my class," he said proudly.

Big Boy couldn't help it—he laughed. Nelle nudged him but found herself giggling too. When they glanced up, Truman was staring at the bush they hid behind.

"Callie isn't here, as you know," said Jenny. "She's been very ill and staying at the rest home, but she sends you her best."

"I'm sure she does," he said, looking past them into the house. "Where's Queenie?" he asked.

"Queenie's out at Big Boy's. He'll come for a visit soon enough," said Jenny.

Truman looked offended. "Sook didn't want to keep her *here?*" he asked, his voice rising.

Bud leaned down and whispered in his ear, "You know Jenny don't much care for dogs."

Nelle pushed Big Boy into view, where he reluctantly piped up. "Don't you worry, Truman," said Big Boy. "I'm taking good care of him—I mean, her?"

Truman didn't say anything. He was watching Nelle.

"Speak of the devil—look, it's Big Boy and Nelle. Say hello, Truman," said Bud, nudging him.

"Hello," he said shyly, staring at the ground.

"Truman, is that how you treat your friends after all this time?" asked Joe.

"Oh, I saw them already, remember?" He quickly glanced at them. "Hello again, Big Boy, Nelle. What do you know?" His voice had always been peculiar, high and soft with a quiet Southern lilt. He spoke like an ethereal angel with a wicked streak, so it was hard to tell if he was serious or not.

Nelle squinted at him, sizing him up. She was still a head taller. "I know you ain't too big for yer britches, that's what I know."

"Hiya, Truman," said Big Boy.

Truman looked him up and down too. "My, Big Boy, how you've grown."

Big Boy smiled. "Have I? It's hard for me to tell since I see myself just about every day."

Nelle rolled her eyes, then got to the point. "How come you haven't written us in five months?" she asked.

Truman didn't seem to have an answer. He wanted to say something, but no words came out. But then Sook called from deep inside the house:

"Trueheart, is that you? Has my little buddy finally come home to visit his Nanny Rumbley for the holidays?"

Suddenly, his demeanor changed. He was like a six-year-old again. His gaze was drawn to the house, where his beloved Sook sat by the dining table, her face lit up by a toothless smile as she held out the lemon meringue pie she'd made especially for him.

As if in a trance, Truman moved past everybody toward her. "My Tru." Sook beamed, almost shaking with joy. She was the eldest of the ancient cousins who lived under Jenny and was wearing her homemade quilted housecoat, a gingham dress, and tennis shoes. Her thin white hair glowed bright in the afternoon sun, her eyes wide open and twice as big behind the Coke-bottle glasses she wore.

Truman gazed upon the lemon meringue pie he'd been dreaming about for ages. But his smile suddenly turned into a frown once he took a closer look.

Nelle could almost feel it coming.

Truman examined the pie closely, ignoring his dear ol' Sook. Suddenly, he stamped his foot. "They're not *tall* enough, Sook," he said, pointing at the peaks of sugary meringue on the pie. "You know I only like lemon meringue pie when the peaks are very, very tall!"

Sook looked confused, her eyes filling with tears. "Uh, I guess . . . I guess I'll just have to make another one—"

"Please see to it, Sook. I've come all this way," he said, frustrated. "All this way for nothing!"

Sook sat there trembling. "I—I just wanted you to be . . . ever so happy." She tried wiping her eyes with her housecoat sleeve while still holding her pie up, but as she did so, some of the meringue slipped off and plopped right into her lap.

That was the last straw.

Nelle rushed Truman from behind, grabbed him by the scruff of his stiff collar, and hauled him through the kitchen.

She pushed him out the back screen door, where he fell, fancy suit and all, onto the dirt behind the house.

"Just who in the heck do you think you are, coming in here and putting on airs in front of us?" She kicked dirt on him, swatting his leg or arm away when he tried to stop her.

"Quit it, Nelle—"

"You think you're better than us, now that you live in *New York City?* How dare you make Sook cry! She spent all morning making that durn pie!"

"Nelle, I'm—"

"An' her and Little Bit decorated the house just for you! Me and Big Boy waited by the road for an hour just to see you!" Her eyes welled up, her face red with hurt. "Just who do you think you are, you—you *shrimp!*"

Truman hated being called a shrimp.

He scrambled out from under her and drew himself up as tall as he could. He started to dust off his suit but saw how hopelessly dirty it was. "Look what you did . . ."

"You had it coming. Now answer me." She glared.

He looked her straight in the eye. "Who do I think I am? I'm Truman Garcia Capote, that's who," he said defiantly.

Nelle blinked. "*Gar-ci-a Ca-po-tee?* What kind of loony-bird talk is that?"

"Truman!" shouted Jenny from the back door. "Come in here at once and apologize to Sook. You made her cry. What's wrong with you, boy?"

"*You've* made her cry plenty," Truman said under his breath.

He shot a look at Nelle. "If you must know, my mother is going to get full custody of me, and Joe will then adopt me and give me his name too! After that, we can finally all live in Manhattan as one big happy family."

"Truman! I'm talking to you!" said Jenny again.

Truman seemed different from the confident little misfit storyteller Nelle had known a couple of years back. He seemed beaten down, defeated almost, but hiding it behind a cool veneer. "And you believe your mom?" asked Nelle. "How is custody going to make it any different than now?"

He seemed unsure but tried to convince himself. "It's different because now, every time she sees me, she thinks of Arch. But with him out of the picture, I'll be her one and only," he said. "And Joe will accept me as his own too."

"Truman, I'm going to count to three . . ." said Jenny.

"I don't know . . ." said Nelle. "Don't you miss being here?"

A shadow of doubt passed over Truman's eyes. "I . . ." was all he said, his thoughts derailed.

"Maybe you're not getting the whole story," said Nelle. "What if there was another way?"

"One . . ." said Jenny.

His eyes flickered. "Another way?"

Nelle leaned in and whispered, "Arch told me to tell you that if he wins, he'll let you live here with Jenny for good."

Truman took a step back. "He's a liar . . . He's desperate because he might be going to jail."

Nelle grimaced. "I hate to break it to you, but your mother ain't so trustworthy herself."

"Two . . ."

Truman rubbed his eyes. "I don't know . . ."

Nelle spoke quicker. "He says if you tell the judge all about the crazy life she leads in New York, he'll win and then he'll give his custody away to Jenny."

"Three—"

"All right!" he said to Jenny. "I'm coming."

Jenny held open the screen door. Inside, Sook was still sobbing.

Truman sighed. "Remember all those stories we used to write together?" he said to Nelle, half smiling.

She nodded, and for a moment, Nelle saw his old self again.

"You were good," he said, looking her in the eye. "How come you stopped?"

She wanted to answer him, to tell him that writing felt impossible without his crazy imagination around to inspire her. But he was starting back up the steps to the porch.

"Isn't it strange that all I ever wanted was to live with my mother, but instead I spent most of my time at a boarding school wishing I were back in Monroeville?"

He gave Nelle a last look, hung his head, and walked inside, where he crawled up into Sook's arms and quieted her tears.

2
Showdown

The Monroe County Courthouse was not only the tallest building in Monroeville, it was also the most impressive and intimidating presence in the town square. It loomed over the whole downtown like a sentry. The old clock, which always ran five minutes slow, marked time for everyone, so the entire town ran five minutes slow too. Not that it mattered. In the South, no one was ever in a hurry—until they were.

Nelle and Big Boy sat in the balcony where the colored folks usually sat. Big Boy had brought along Queenie, Truman's rat terrier that Jenny had disowned. He thought it would be a good surprise for Truman on what would surely be a very strange day.

Nobody bothered them in the balcony because colored folks and dogs were generally treated as one and the same: they were tolerated as long as they knew their place. Nelle preferred the balcony because they were left to their own devices. The people up there knew Nelle's father to be a decent man, and any daughter of his was okay by them. The only thing she didn't like was when they would stand aside to let her pass. That was how black people deferred to any white person. Didn't matter if it was a kid or an elder.

It was rare that any court proceeding drew a crowd. Most people thought legal matters were on the boring side; Nelle found them to be a fascinating peek into other people's lives. But today was different.

Despite the family's best efforts to keep things quiet, the town turned out for this one. Arch had spent the day spreading rumors about Nina's lurid life in New York and her sordid history with men. Had Joe not been around to hold her back, she would have clocked Arch right there in the courtroom, something he would have loved.

"Never get in the ring with someone who has nothing to lose" was the last thing Arch said when he spotted Nina heading into the courthouse. If looks could kill, Nina's stare would have sent a death ray into Arch's brain.

The crowd was restless and eager for things to get started. It reminded Nelle of the snake fight she'd seen with Truman — one lethal viper pitted against another. Both were vicious, and despite it being close to the holidays, the crowd wanted a fight to the end.

The kicker was the prize: Truman.

Jenny took control of the situation and held Truman's hand all the way into the courthouse gallery. Jenny gave both parents the evil eye, even though she secretly liked the idea of Truman returning to Monroeville for good.

For some reason, she had dressed Truman in a baby-blue suit with a matching hat and tie. He looked like a little prince. He sat in the front row in the middle, trying not to favor either side. Everyone stared at this peculiar bird. Nelle and Big Boy just felt sorry for him.

"It's kinda strange seeing Truman down there like that," said Nelle. "He always talked about one day being the key witness in a big case—and now he is."

"Yeah, but he always wanted to be a part of a murder case. Only no one is ever killed around here," said Big Boy.

"I sure as heck don't know how he's gonna get out of this pickle," said Nelle.

Big Boy shrugged. "Well, Bud always used to say that boy could get out of a sticky situation quicker than a worm digging through mud in a summer rain."

Truman's gaze floated up to the balcony and he twisted his head until he saw Nelle and Big Boy. Nelle waved at him, but it wasn't until Big Boy held up Queenie that Truman's face lit up with joy. Queenie began yapping, so Big Boy had to hide him again, but he knew that he'd made Truman smile for the first time since he'd come back.

Nelle saw the crowd down below whispering behind Truman's back. He was trying awfully hard to ignore them. In the balcony, folks were talking mostly about Lillie Mae. Many had experienced her scorn at one time or another. If black people had been allowed to testify, Lillie Mae would have been in trouble. Most of them felt for Arch, being down on his luck and struggling to stay afloat. That they could relate to, even if they didn't care for him personally.

"What do you think he's gonna say?" asked Nelle.

"Knowing Truman, something that'll get him in trouble," said Big Boy.

Old crotchety Judge Fountain seemed disturbed by the large turnout. His bushy eyebrows cast a shadow over his eyes as he banged his gavel.

"I'll remind everybody here that this is a civil matter, *not* a criminal trial," he said in a voice that sounded like sandpaper. "Because it is the holiday season and there are children present, I'll ask everyone to watch their language. I expect y'all to act accordingly or I'll boot you out faster than a rooster chasing a hen."

At one table sat Nina and Joe, looking dapper but not extravagant. They held hands, an ideal churchgoing couple, except they weren't. A.C. looked uneasy sitting next to them in his rumpled suit.

Across the way sat Arch, hair slicked back, dressed in what was once an impeccable three-piece suit, now past its prime. His lawyer, Mr. Ratcliff, a behemoth of a man squeezed into trousers one size too small, was an ambulance chaser always looking for a quick buck.

The judge spoke again: "All righty, now, ladies, gentlemen. We are here to discuss the custody of the child Truman Streckfus Persons." The judge glanced up at Truman, who didn't know if he should stand or not. "From the parents, Lillie Mae Persons and Julian Archulus Persons—"

"Objection, Your Honor," said Nina out loud. A.C. tried to hush her, but she persisted. "The name is Nina Capote— Your . . . Judgeship." She stood and curtsied.

"Is that your legal name now, Lillie Mae?" asked the judge.

Joe stood. "Yes, Your Honor, she is now my wife. It is our desire that once custody is granted, I will adopt Truman formally and seek a name change: Truman Garcia Capote," he said proudly.

Arch laughed out loud. "My son is no New York dago, I'll tell you that—"

Joe took offense. "I am Cuban, sir, not whatever a *dago* is—"

"A dago is any dark-skinned foreigner who don't know that you shouldn't name a white kid Garcia—"

The judge banged his gavel. "Order! The next person to speak out of turn is going to get this gavel upside their head."

A.C. pulled on Joe's sleeve, forcing him to sit.

The judge continued. "Now, I have before me all kinds of reports pertaining to Mrs. Capote and her to-dos up in New York."

Arch guffawed at Nina. "You have the one about her having a fling with that boxer Jack Dempsey?"

"That is a *lie!*" protested Nina. "And besides, Arch was the one who put me up to flirting with him in the first place, because he wanted to be his promoter—"

"That's enough." The judge trained his eyes on the both of them. "In addition, I have here a rather lengthy list of arrest reports on Mr. Persons—"

"Ha!" said Nina.

Mr. Ratcliff stood up. "All foolish charges, Your Honor— and he was acquitted of most."

The judge shook his head and swore under his breath. "What a fine pair y'all make. I should annul your divorce just to punish you *both*."

A murmur ran through the gallery. Both A.C. and the ambulance chaser strenuously objected, but clearly the crowd loved it.

The judge banged his gavel again. "Order. Look, I enjoy a good smear campaign as much as the next man, but who I really want to hear from is the child. Truman!"

Jenny nudged him to stand.

The judge waved him up. "Well, come on, boy. Sit in the stand—" He suddenly seemed to notice Truman's clothes. "What is that you're wearing? You look like a peacock."

Truman knew all eyes were on him. "It's from New York. It's the latest fashion." He walked calmly up to the judge as if he were pintsize royalty. "Where do I take my oath, Your Honor?" he said in a voice so high it drifted off into the ether. Nelle smiled. She used to say that he had a voice only a dog could hear.

The judge pointed to the witness chair. "This ain't a criminal trial, boy. Have a seat."

Truman looked at the American flag standing behind the judge and raised his right hand anyway. "I swear to tell the truth, and nothing but," he said very quickly before the judge could object.

Fountain rolled his eyes. "Fine, son. Now that you are 'under oath,' why don't you take a seat and tell us what it's been like living up in New York City."

"Well," Truman said as he sat. Nelle could almost see him rifling through his brain for which of the hundreds of tales he wanted to spill. "New York is a strange and wondrous place. Did you know there are twenty bridges, thirty thousand taxicab drivers, eighteen tunnels, and both underground subways *and* elevated trains?"

"You don't say?" said the judge, humoring him.

"I do say." Now Truman was talking to the crowd. "There are also alligators in the sewer and skyscrapers as high as the sky."

"Have you seen King Kong?" someone in the gallery shouted, to everyone's laughter.

"No," he said, smiling. "But everything there *is* bigger—the movie houses are like palaces, Yankee Stadium is like the Roman Colosseum, even the parks are enormous. Why, Central Park is bigger than Monroeville itself. And the library! Four stories of books with giant stone lions guarding the front doors!"

The crowd was agape in wonderment.

"That's all fine, Truman," said the judge. "But what I really want to know is, what's it like living *with Nina and Joe* in New York City?"

"Oh," he said thoughtfully. "Well . . . when I'm not away at school, on weekends I live in a very nice apartment right on Park Avenue. *The* Park Avenue," he added for emphasis. "My stepfather, Joe, spoils us, says we should never be wanting for anything."

"Does your mama cook for you?" asked the judge.

"Oh, heavens, *no!* We go out to fancy restaurants and the like. The Stork Club or El Morocco, places like that."

"Aren't those nightclubs?" asked the judge.

Truman pondered the question. "Well, if you mean do they have music and drinking, then I suppose yes. But the food is really the best. There's nothing like that here in Monroeville, I can tell you that. Even the gangsters eat there."

The crowd stirred. "The gangsters?" asked Judge Fountain.

Truman nodded. "I saw Lucky Luciano in there once. He had some blond moll with him. You know, a gun moll? A *dame*. That's what Mother calls them, though she uses other words sometimes. Anyhow, New York's a very exciting place. They have parties almost every night. Dukes and duchesses like to call on Mother. She's quite the society gal."

The judge lowered his glasses. "Tell me, do they ever leave you alone?"

Truman paused and reluctantly said, "Sometimes, yes. I

don't like that. It reminds me of when I was two and we were living in a hotel in New Orleans. She and Arch would go out at night and lock me in. I remember kicking and screaming at the door until—"

"Your Honor," said A.C. "I think we need to get to the basic question, which is whether Truman wants to live with his mother or his father. I think we all know Mr. Persons has been spreading innuendo about Truman's mother to make her out to be some kind of horrible person, when all the while Arch has never paid child support or even shown up for his three months of custody a year. And in fact, as we speak, he is awaiting trial for forgery that might send him to Angola Prison—"

"Objection, Your Honor," said Mr. Ratcliff, puffing out his chest. "My client is just trying to find the best place for his child to live. He knows he's no saint and is not applying for full custody for his own sake. But what he *is* saying is that Truman's mother is *also* unfit, and therefore, Truman should stay *here,* in Monroeville, with his cousin Jenny!"

A murmur ran through the crowd. Jenny sat up, trying to look as dignified as she could.

Ratcliff continued. "She and the cousins had done a fine and proper job of raising Truman until his mother suddenly decided she wanted her child again. We all know it was just to get back at my client. Perhaps we should cut the malarkey and ask Truman where he prefers to live? After all, Jenny, Sook, and the rest are his *real* family."

The judge sat back and nodded. "Well, son, given living with your mother in New York or staying here with your cousins, which would *you* prefer?"

Truman looked out on the gallery. His mother and stepdad held hands and sat with bated breath. Arch was smiling, nodding at his son like he knew what he had to say. Then there was Jenny, trying to remain stoic, pleading with her eyes. Finally, his gaze drifted nervously up to the balcony where Nelle and Big Boy sat.

"I know these things are never easy, son," said the judge. "If you weigh the pros and cons . . . Both have the means to take care of you. Maybe you feel more suited for the small-town life in the South rather than big-city living."

Truman stared at his shoes. "I think I would like to live with . . ." His gaze wandered the gallery again, searching for answers, but finally he couldn't hold back. "My mother."

"Yes!" Nina jumped up and hugged Joe. She glared over her husband's shoulder at Arch, who had to be held back by Mr. Ratcliff. A shouting match ensued. Jenny just shook her head and walked out of the gallery, clearly full of disappointment. Truman glanced up at Nelle and Big Boy again and shrugged.

"Well, that's that," said Big Boy.

Nelle sighed. "I guess we won't be getting any presents for him after all."

The judge ruled for full custody for Tru's mother, Nina. In addition, he granted Joe the right to adopt Truman and formally change his name to Truman Garcia Capote, the last nail in the coffin for Arch.

Arch slunk back to New Orleans to lick his wounds.

Wishing to avoid any more gossip, Nina, Joe, and Truman left the courthouse and hit the road back to New York.

There would be no Christmas with Truman. Nelle and Big Boy would not see him again for another two years.

Five Days Before Christmas, 1937

3
Return of the Prodigal Son

The hobo, Fancy Bob, threw open the boxcar door, sending the wind and cold ripping through Truman's body as the freight train roared into Monroe County.

"You awake now, boy?" shouted Fancy Bob.

Truman had been awake since he'd hopped aboard the train outside New York two days before. He wrapped the cardboard around him tighter to keep the chill out but to little effect. "Where are we?" he shouted over the thundering noise of the tracks.

Bob's hair whipped about in the wind, his one good eye staring out at the passing landscape. He looked worn and weary, like the other train hoppers who filled the boxcar. "Coming up on Monroeville—or at least, as close as these tracks get," Bob yelled. "When she comes through the crossing, that's when you gotta jump."

"Jump?" Truman looked at Bob like he was crazy. "You mean . . . it's not going to stop in Evergreen?"

Fancy Bob laughed. "This here's a freight train, boy, not the *Midnight Special* out of Baltimore. When I say *jump*, you *jump!*"

The icy wind howled all around Truman as he watched the blur of the ground fly by. He was shocked at how cold it was. He wasn't sure what was worse: not having winter clothes on or knowing that he'd be smashed to smithereens when he hit the ground.

He looked around at the other freight hoppers who'd traveled from one end of the Eastern Seaboard to the other, desperately looking for work or trying to escape from the past. He fit in with the latter; he felt a kinship with Idaho Willie, 10 Tooth Slim, and Porkpie Johnson. They were all on the run, just like him.

Fancy Bob looked ahead down the tracks. "Don't worry, boy. She slows down at the crossing, and after she passes the road, it's all sand. Just keep your feet together, tuck in, and roll. You gotta lose the box, though!"

Truman had wrapped himself in cardboard all night to block out the freezing wind. He let it go and the cardboard took flight like a giant moth careening around the inside of the boxcar until—*whoosh!*—it was sucked right out the side door, vanishing into the early-morning sky.

Fancy Bob stared at Truman's military dress uniform, which

he hadn't seen when he climbed aboard the train outside Atlanta. "Why you dressed like a soldier, boy? They letting babies join up now, are they?"

Truman straightened his cadet attire: gray suit with brass buttons and a braided rope aiguillette on each shoulder. He had to think fast. "If you must know, I'm a spy on a secret mission. President Roosevelt himself personally assigned me to the job because I look like I'm thirteen. But I'm really twenty-one."

Bob rubbed his one good eye. "You don't say? Don't you think if you're dressed like that, you'll stand out?"

He looked down at his polished dress shoes. "Of course. That's why I'm meeting up at a secret rendezvous at oh-eight-hundred hours, in the woods. They'll have my undercover clothes ready."

Fancy Bob scratched his noggin. "And what's so important in Monroeville that President Roosevelt sent *you* during Christmas week?"

Truman blinked. "It's a secret," he said.

Fancy Bob cackled and had a swig of shinny. He took a close look at Truman's polished brass buttons, which bore the words *St. John's Military Academy* on them. "You wouldn't be one of them lads escaping from a military boys' school or something like that, would you?"

Truman sucked in his breath. The boxcar jolted, the train wheels squealing as it began to slow down.

He looked out the sliding door. The early-morning light

burned orange on the surrounding forests and barren fields. Truman could almost smell Monroeville from here; it was a strange concoction of cotton, sweet tea, fireplaces, and chocolate-scented vines. But the most overwhelming smell at this time of year was pine, as in the Christmas-tree forests that had sprung up around the county.

Fancy Bob nodded as he spotted the dirt road coming up. "Yup," he said. "This is it."

Truman was having second thoughts. About running away, about his future, about jumping. Fancy Bob put his hand on Truman's shoulder. "Don't worry, lad, your secret's safe with me. I've run away more than once in my life. Never had a proper home but for the rails. Take it from me: Go home if you got one. I wish I did."

And with that, Fancy Bob pushed Truman off the train.

"Tuck and roll!" he shouted as Truman hit the sandy dirt off the tracks.

Despite his years of gymnastics, Truman took two steps and hit the dirt face first, coming to a skidding stop in a puff of red dust. He rolled over on his side, gasping for breath, as the freight train sped up again and disappeared down the tracks.

I must be cursed, he thought. A curse was the only explanation Truman could think of to cause such a run of bad luck and ill fortune.

Lying there in the dirt as the brutal cold slowly crept through every pore in his body, Truman felt that everything had gone wrong since he'd left Monroeville. Only a curse would turn his

mother against him. She'd gone to all those lengths to get custody, then did an about-face, suddenly acting like she didn't want
him after all. She was constantly bemoaning all his quirks: his
funny high voice, the way he sashayed when he walked, the eccentric clothing he wore, and the artsy boys he befriended.

Mother had finally had it with him. "I wish I'd given birth to
Pinocchio! At least he turned into a *real* boy in the end!"

"Pinocchio isn't real, he's *fiction!*" was all Truman could
think of to say (he was a writer, after all).

Her answer was to ship him off to St. John's Military
Academy for Boys, of all places. The academy was about an hour
north of Manhattan and had a reputation for reforming even the
toughest of delinquents. However, no cadet had ever been more
ill-suited than delicate little Truman; even Joe shook his head
when they dropped him off.

"Sorry, son. Your mother's mind is made up. It's out of my
hands," he'd said.

Every day Truman was bullied at the academy and every
week Mother refused to visit or even listen to his complaints, the
curse weighed heavier on him. Finally, his only choice was to run
far away, hoping his curse wouldn't follow.

The only place he could think to go was Monroeville.

He just wanted to see Sook again, to have Queenie lick his
face, to eat Little Bit's butter beans, to hear Bud tell him jokes
on the front porch, even to have Jenny lecture him. He missed
them all.

But mostly, he missed Big Boy and Nelle.

He groaned as he got up and, in a daze, started trudging along aimlessly. He wasn't thinking straight, walking into the woods instead of down the road. But his mind was foggy. He had no gloves and had lost his cap during his escape. His fine blond hair, cut short by the sergeant at arms to make him appear manlier, offered no protection from the cold. His ears were pink, his lips chapped, his nose runny. His teeth chattered like the telegraph he used to practice Morse code at the academy. His knees and elbows were scraped and sore. And his stomach gurgled and protested at having lived off only half a loaf of bread he'd swiped before he ran away.

After half an hour of wandering in the bitter cold, he just felt like lying back down on the frigid ground and closing his eyes. So he did.

It might have been a dream or maybe some kind of vision. In Truman's mind, it was Christmas Day. People were gathered next to a fireplace, presents on the floor, hot apple cider in hands. Everyone was there: Sook, Jenny, Bud, and Queenie. Nelle and Big Boy sat on either side of him, stringing popcorn onto a fishing line. Truman gushed with a warmth he'd never felt before. It was a perfect family moment.

"A tree should be twice as tall as a boy," said Sook. "So's he cain't steal the star!"

Truman looked past her and saw a Christmas tree. It seemed so real, perfect in every way, its handmade star wrapped in tinfoil shining by the light of the fire, its magnificent branches displaying all the ornaments he and Sook had created over the years.

Suddenly, he felt that tree made everything okay. With a tree like that, his curse would go cowering into the night. A tree like that announced a fresh start, a magical Christmas to beat all Christmases. A tree like that erased the past.

When he opened his eyes again, he saw it—not a vision or a dream, but a magnificent cedar standing right before him in the forest: the perfect Christmas tree.

4
The Dress

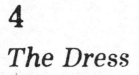

I hate it," muttered Nelle. She hadn't worn a dress since she was five and the mere thought of it had driven her to a life of overalls and bare feet.

"Hush," said her older sister Bear as she looked Nelle over in the bedroom mirror. Bear was a no-nonsense woman now, working under A.C. in the law office. It was like having a third parent. "Mama needs something to feel good about this Christmas, and I'm tired of hearing her talk about how she wishes you were a proper girl."

"I'm proper enough," Nelle said. She looked around the bedroom she and Bear and their other sister, Weezie, had all shared growing up. As in the rest of the house, everything here was frugal and unadorned: beds painted white, no rugs to clean, wood floors rubbed with oil.

"If mules were proper, you'd be queen," Bear said, buttoning the back of Nelle's Christmas dress. "Fortunately, they're not, and the only queen around here is the one they crown at the hog festival. Besides, you're becoming a young woman whether you like it or not. Might as well dress like one."

Bear smoothed the shoulders of the red velvet dress she'd made by repurposing an old curtain from the now-closed movie house. With its white collar and belt, the dress made Nelle look like one of Santa's helpers.

"Phooey." Nelle looked at herself in the mirror. *Nelle Harper Lee in a Christmas dress?* It was surely cold enough outside— maybe hell *had* frozen over. "Who in their right mind would wear such a thing?" she said, tugging on it.

"You." Bear took Nelle's hair out of its ponytail and let it fall to her shoulders.

"Don't," Nelle said, fighting her off.

Bear slapped at her hand. "Don't be so afraid to look pretty. Who knows, a boy might *actually* like you one day. And you look good with longer hair."

"Well, I don't like it. It just gets tangled all the time and gets in the way of everything. I don't know why Mama won't let me cut it."

"Because she wants you to not stick out like a sore thumb," said Bear. "Being a tomboy is okay when you're little. But you're almost twelve and getting bigger. Soon, you might even need to wear a br—"

"Don't say it!" Nelle glared.

"Fine," said Bear, sitting back. "I'm just suggesting that, with a little makeup, you might not look *half* bad."

Nelle stared daggers. "If you ever see me wearing lipstick, you can just shoot me," she said, grimacing at the mirror. "Besides, no boys like me."

"Truman liked you."

Nelle rolled her eyes. "He's not . . . like the rest of 'em."

Bear threw her hands in the air. "Maybe if you didn't beat up the boys constantly . . ."

Nelle shrugged. "Well, they're stupid. They deserve it half the time—"

Suddenly, Nelle's eye caught something moving in the mirror. She swung around and stared at the darkened window behind Bear.

"What is it?" asked Bear.

"Nothin'. I just thought I saw . . ."

Nelle walked up to the window, where she could feel the chill leaking in through the cracks. There was nothing but the darkness of night outside. "Just a reflection, I guess."

She didn't want to say what she thought she saw, because it was downright foolish. She peered into the dark. Was that a figure across the yard by the horse-bone fence?

"Turn the light off," she said.

"What? Why?" asked Bear.

The Dress

Nelle walked over and shut the lamp off, then returned to the window. Everything seemed the same under the foggy moonlight: Jenny's house, the wall, the double chinaberry tree that held the fort —

Now she must be seeing things — was that a soldier standing under the tree? A blond soldier —

"*Boo!*" Bear grabbed Nelle from behind. Nelle tried not to act scared.

Bear scoffed. "You and your ghosts," she said. "Come on, let's go show Mama that dress. You can wear it to church on Christmas Day," she said, heading out of the room.

Fat chance, Nelle thought as she stared out at the night. She put her hand on the window and pulled it back immediately. It was as cold as ice.

"In a minute," she said.

Alone in her room, Nelle could see Jenny's house across the way. In one window sat Jenny at a desk, going through her ledgers by candlelight. In another, Little Bit, their part Cajun, part Indian, part black cook, was stoking Ol' Buckeye, the massive stove that filled their kitchen. Callie's room remained dark after her sudden death from cancer the previous summer. That was so sad, especially because not many people had liked her except her family. And even then she was not beloved. Bud was in his room huddled over a steaming pot of herbal vapors to help his asthma. And last, Sook sat by herself, cutting out pictures from magazines and saving them in an overflowing box so that she could show Truman whenever he decided to visit again.

Nelle's eyes wandered over to the chinaberry tree that held her and Truman's treehouse. She stared at the cutout window and swore she could almost see someone up there.

She instinctively reached for the string-can telephone that connected her room to the fort and to Truman's old room. She held the can to her ear and listened. Nothing.

"Truman?" she whispered.

No one answered. She put down the can and headed to the living room. When she was gone, the can suddenly moved and fell to the ground.

5
Hideout

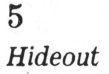

Truman sat in his old treehouse, staring at the tin-can phone. The sight of Nelle in a dress with long hair had thrown him for a loop. For all he knew, she'd have the same reaction when she saw him dressed like a military cadet: *Who are you?*

When she'd held up the can to her ear, he'd almost spoken to her. But what would he have said? *I ran away? I'm AWOL? My mother was crazy for thinking she could send me to military school?*

Truman wished he could have cut down that Christmas tree and dragged it back to Jenny's, but he didn't have an ax and there was no way he could have lugged it home by himself. He needed Big Boy's and maybe Bud's help. So he'd claimed it by tying his red academy belt around the base of the trunk so he could find it later and make everything okay again.

He drew his collar tight against his neck to try to keep warm. He wanted to take off his stupid uniform and burn it, but he didn't have any other clothes. Truman looked around and found an old, thin blanket, which he wrapped around himself. He didn't care if there were spiders or boll weevils in it; he needed warmth.

The moonlight was just bright enough for him to see that the books in the treehouse were dusty and falling apart. Some of his old trinkets were still on the shelf: a couple of jacks, an old pipe, a magnifying glass (cracked), and a collection of rocks and leaves. On the wall he spotted his old Sherlock Holmes deerstalker cap. He reached for it, swatted the dust off, and plopped it on his head.

It was too small. Had his head grown? Or had the hat shrunk? He pulled on it hard and the bill just ripped off in his hands. So much for Sherlock.

A firefly floated aimlessly through the opening in the fort and settled on the edge of the blanket. Only it wasn't a firefly. When the spot where it landed began to smoke, he realized it was a burning ember.

"Hey!" he said, tapping it out with his shoe.

Then he saw another. And another.

He swatted them out of the air or blew them out the other side window.

When Truman looked around to see where they were coming from, he spotted A.C. Lee in his living room overloading the fireplace with old dogwood. Even from the treehouse, Truman could see the wood popping and sparking into a huge bonfire. He saw the embers flying out the top of their chimney.

Nelle's mother was playing the piano by the fire. She looked like she hadn't slept in a week, and Truman realized he hadn't slept in a couple of days either.

Then Nelle walked in. Or, rather, she was pushed in by her sister Bear. He could see Nelle pushing back. A.C. glanced over his shoulder and smiled but probably knew better than to say anything.

When her mother saw Nelle, she stopped playing and threw her arms wide. Nelle reluctantly walked into her embrace, only to have the life squeezed out of her. Nelle tried to squirm out until she realized her mother was crying. Not just crying, but sobbing. Nelle melted into her arms and hugged her back. A.C. came over and offered words.

Truman felt sorry for her mother, for she suffered from melancholia, a deep-rooted neurosis that caused her to behave erratically when she was depressed. She was known as a kind woman who liked to knit and play piano but also as an eccentric who'd stand on the front porch and shout advice to passersby on how to walk properly. But Truman had his own problems at the moment.

The embers were really sailing past his window now. He followed them with his eyes as they glided toward Jenny's house. The house stood exactly as he'd remembered it: a rambling wood building surrounded by a wraparound porch, a picket fence, and Jenny's flower bushes.

All the lights had gone out in Jenny's house except one. Jenny was still working away on the books in the front room. Truman was afraid to talk to her. As much as she looked out for him, the idea of giving up on school or blaming some curse for his troubles would go against her grain.

He heard a door slam and spun around to see Nelle fall onto her bed. She started punching at her pillow; her face was red with anger and sorrow.

Suddenly, she sat up, her eyes scanning the room looking for something. She ran from drawer to drawer, opening and shutting them until she found what she was looking for.

Scissors.

Nelle held the scissors in her hand and stared at herself in the mirror. She hated her dress, hated her hair, and hated herself for hating them.

"Why can't I just be normal like all the other girls?" she asked herself, even though the idea repelled her.

She grabbed a handful of hair and held it out, then positioned the scissors to cut the whole thing off. That was when she heard a tap on the window.

She turned and dropped the scissors. The ghost of Truman had returned.

Maybe she stood there a little too long gaping at him, because Truman began hopping in place to keep warm. When she realized how cold he was outside, she ran for the window and forced it open. The icy wind made her catch her breath. Her bare legs prickled from the cold, but she didn't care. They both stood there, staring into some alternate universe where Truman dressed as a soldier and Nelle dressed like a girl.

She could see his lips turning blue. "Well, you just gonna stand there or are you gonna come in?" she asked.

He nodded. "I wasn't sure it was you," he said through chattering teeth. She blushed, embarrassed that he was seeing her like this.

"I was thinking the same thing," she said quietly.

He crawled in through the window, but one of the rope aiguillettes that decorated his uniform caught on the latch. He hung there, trying to reach back to unhook himself. Nelle stepped in and yanked on it to no avail. Finally, she just cut the rope with the scissors and in he stumbled.

She pulled the window closed and shivered as the chill slowly left her body. Truman got up and dusted himself off, frowning at the cut rope before he realized that he didn't really care.

They stood a couple of feet apart, staring at each other as if they had both escaped from a costume ball. They felt like strangers.

Finally, Truman couldn't help it—he laughed.

"What's so funny?" Nelle said, and then she started laughing too. "Have *you* looked in a mirror lately?"

"Believe me, as soon as I can, I'm going to burn these clothes," he said, tugging on his sleeves.

"Good." She chuckled. "Then I won't have to do it for you. Did you run off and join the army or a marching band?"

"I don't know—did you run away from the North Pole?"

Nelle stopped laughing and Truman thought he'd gone too far. An awkward moment passed and then she broke out laughing again and so did he.

When the giggles subsided, they both looked down at their feet. Truman was wearing his once-shiny cadet shoes, now caked with red mud, and Nelle was wearing red wool socks with Santas on them.

After an uncomfortable ten seconds, they both spoke:

"What are you doing—"

"Were you going to cut your—"

They stopped, then: "You first—" they said at the same time. "Jinx."

Nelle jumped in. "What are you doing here? And why are you dressed like . . . *that?*"

Truman began to say something, then paused. "You can't tell anyone."

Nelle nodded slowly.

Truman chose his words carefully. "It all started because—I was kicked out of that God-awful boarding school. They said I was failing because I was lazy and easily distracted and—"

He noticed an old poster of a lady in a bonnet and old-fashioned blue dress. "Who's that?"

"Jane Austen. She's a *writer*. You were saying?" asked Nelle.

Truman kept staring at the picture. "Doesn't she write those girly—"

"She is one of the finest writers that ever lived. Now get on with it," she said impatiently. "You were saying 'easily distracted' . . ."

"Yes," he agreed. "Well, they also said I was causing too much distraction for others because of all my outspokenness."

"What else is new?" she said.

"Exactly. Anyway, they said I'd never amount to anything, which got Mother really upset, especially when they said I should be psychiatrically evaluated."

"You mean, like, see a *shrink?*"

"Well, not exactly. There were these university types doing some kind of study on what makes a great student and they had me take an IQ test." He stood up straight and puffed out his chest. "Turns out I'm a genius."

"A genius."

"Yep. Certified, too. In fact, I had the highest score in the state of New York."

Same old Truman, Nelle thought. She could smell a Truman story a mile away.

"So they sent me to a special school, an academy. Called St. John's," he said.

She looked him up and down. He was wearing a dark gray wool military outfit with shoulder epaulets and brass buttons. "You mean you were sent to military school? *You?*"

Truman started marching in place. "Why not me? It's more like a school for future officers. Best and the brightest, they say. Besides, they had horses."

"Uh-huh," she said, thinking. "And why are you showing up in the middle of the night? Are Nina and Joe here?"

He stopped marching. "No, I came on my own. They took a trip to Cuba to go visit his family, but I wanted to come here. So I took the train down."

"How come Sook didn't mention it? I saw her this morning," she said.

Truman thought quickly. "Oh, it's a surprise visit. Last-minute."

"She doesn't know? You still haven't been over there?" She glanced out the window and saw that the house had gone dark. "Well, everyone's gone to bed now. What are you waiting for? And where are all your things?"

Truman always got a certain look in his eyes when he was cornered. He started getting defensive and looking for a diversion, just like Arch always did.

"My bags are outside. I just wanted to say hi, is all. Is that okay?" he said. "Meanwhile, why didn't you write to tell me you were a girl now? I would have brought flowers."

Nelle was not amused.

Truman changed the subject. He was sweating something fierce all of a sudden. "Why's it so hot in here? I think A.C. is burning down a forest."

Nelle knew better than to press him. She eased up. "Well,

you might as well spend the night. You can see them in the morning—"

Right then, they heard a scream, followed by footsteps running. Nelle's mother was at it again, laughing or crying hysterically; Truman couldn't tell.

Nelle sighed. "Hold on, I'll be right back," she said, heading for the door. "Don't go anywhere."

Truman watched her disappear down the hallway, then decided to crawl back out the window into the frozen night.

6
Sook

The bitter north wind blew through Truman, and he hurried around to the back of Jenny's house. He just wanted to get inside to get warm again. He crept quietly up to the screen door that led into the kitchen. The night felt bleak, broken only by the embers from Nelle's fireplace floating overhead like orange glow bugs lost in the night.

The back door creaked when you opened it, so Truman swung it open quickly. When it still squealed, it brought a small smile to his face. Even better, as soon as he set foot in the kitchen, all the smells came rushing back—the chicory coffee, the herbs Sook grew in the window box, the scent of smoked ham hanging in the pantry. He was taking it all in when he heard the sound of little scampering feet charging toward him.

"Queenie!" he whispered as his old rat terrier leaped into his arms. He stumbled back onto his rear and Queenie attacked his face with licks of love. Truman hugged him with all his might. "What are you doing here? I thought Jenny banned you!" he whispered in the dog's ear. "Oh, Queenie, you didn't forget me, you didn't forget me . . ."

After several minutes of hugging his dog, he was all licked out. Truman set Queenie down and tiptoed toward the first door off the kitchen — Sook's room. He put his ear to the door and could hear her gently wheezing.

Down the hall he could see all the bedrooms. Truman paused by cousin Callie's old room, which bore a black cross and a flower on it. He'd gotten a letter from her shortly before she died, asking forgiveness for all the punishment she'd doled out to him as his teacher. He'd still held a grudge and didn't write her back, but when he heard she'd passed, he felt terrible. He wallowed in sadness for a whole month.

"I forgive you," he whispered to her door, "if you forgive me."

He could smell the herbal remedy coming from Bud's room. So many times he had hidden in there when Jenny or Callie was after him for some misdeed. They would come knocking and Bud would just say, "My backside to you!" and send them off.

At the end of the hall was a double-doored entryway to a room that used to be a parlor but now belonged to Jenny. Beyond that was the magnificent dining room with its high ceilings and pillars, walls of bookshelves, and glass display cases full of Jenny's fineries.

Truman returned to Sook's door and slowly pushed it open with Queenie at his feet—and there it was, the bedroom he'd shared with Sook for the best part of his childhood.

A lantern burned dimly on a side table. He noticed that his bed was gone. Still, he smiled because there was Sook, sound asleep. Her hair seemed whiter, and she appeared a bit thinner, her deep wrinkles making her look a little like Abe Lincoln's missing sister. But what she was holding caught his breath—his old granny-square blanket, the one she'd made for him out of a quilt when he was a baby. He'd been inseparable from that blanket for many years and seeing it again warmed his heart.

He blew out the lantern and crawled into Sook's bed and snuggled up to her and his old blanket, Queenie nestled at his feet. He lay there in the dark staring at her for a few minutes. Then she stirred.

"Trueheart, is that you?" she mumbled.

"Yes, Sook, it's me."

"Where have you been? I stayed up late. I thought we were going to make kites in the attic tonight . . ."

He smiled at the memory. "I missed you, Sook."

"Do you know what time it is?" she whispered.

"It's the middle of the night, Sook."

She made a smacking sound with her mouth. "It's fruitcake time. We need our rest so we can make fruitcakes for Christmas."

Fruitcakes. For years, every Christmas, they would spend days making fruitcakes for everyone, including the president. "I got one from you last year. I ate it all by myself," he said.

"That's right, dear, you always get first dibs . . ."

He lay there for the longest time, glad to be home, dreaming of fruitcakes and trees and all things Christmas. He had a feeling in his heart that maybe the curse had finally left him, that all the bad luck that had followed him would lose his scent now that he was home.

And with that, he fell asleep in her arms, just like old times.

7
Fire!

Truman kicked off the covers. He felt feverish and restless. He hated when Sook closed all the doors and windows in summer. She was afraid that swamp fever would creep in through the screens, and her solution was to batten down the hatches. The only strange thing, he thought when he stirred, was that it was winter.

His eyes shot open, and the bitterness of the smoke choked his eyes. The ceiling glowed orange, and after he wiped his eyes clear, he saw that it was on fire!

He sat up in a panic. Someone was pounding on the front door. Queenie was hysterical, running around the floor, barking up a storm. In the distance, he heard the town siren go off.

"Sook!" he cried.

She was still asleep, or so it appeared, with her mouth wide open and her eyes closed. She wasn't breathing.

He shook her but she didn't wake up. "Sook!" he screamed.

Her eyes popped open and she started hacking from all the smoke. "T-T-Truman?"

"You're alive!" He grabbed her and held on tight. Her nightgown was wet with sweat.

"Of course I'm alive, silly." She pushed him away to look at him. "What are you doing here? Oh, how I've missed you!" She pulled him back into a bear hug.

Then she noticed that the ceiling was on fire.

"Oh my! Is this a dream?"

The bedroom door burst open and Bud stood there in his long johns. "Sook! The house is on fire, let's go—" He froze when he saw Truman and broke out in a grin. "Little Chappie, what are *you* doing here?"

Queenie shot out the door, yapping, at full speed. "We need to get Sook out of here, quick!" Truman tried to help her to the edge of the bed so she could sit up, but she couldn't get over the fact that he was here.

"Why are you dressed like a porter?" asked Sook.

"He ain't a porter, he's a soldier," said Bud, surprised. "Ain't you a little young to be joining up?"

Truman's eyes were burning from the smoke. "I'll explain later. Help me get Sook up!" he said.

"Oh! Sure thing, Truman!" He and Bud each took an elbow and lifted Sook to her feet. "Never thought I'd see *you* in uniform," said Bud.

Truman was coughing hard. "Me neither."

There was a loud *pop!* and the window splintered from the sweltering heat. "Well, I guess we best git!" yelled Bud.

They made it out of the room just as the window exploded, glass shattering everywhere. The kitchen was full of smoke, which burned everyone's throats. Truman shut his mouth tight as they made their way through the kitchen by sense memory.

Finally, they emerged onto the back porch, coughing, and felt their way down the steps. The night air was brutally cold, and because they were without coats, the sweat from the fire instantly chilled them to the bone.

"My eyes!" cried Sook.

Truman looked around for some water and spotted the goldfish pond a few yards away. He crawled over on his hands and knees and plunged his face through a thin layer of frost. It was ice cold, but the water soothed his stinging eyes. He searched his pockets and almost cried when he found he'd saved his granny-square blanket. He soaked it in the water.

He rolled over to Sook and wrung the quilted cloth into her eyes and wiped them clear. Bud was hardly doing better, but he was wiping his face with his sweat-stained shirt. As Truman held the cloth to Sook's eyes, he searched around for Jenny.

The whole backyard was lit up by a blaze of orange light. The wind-driven flames roared to life as volunteer firemen pushed the old fire truck up the back alley. The engine had frozen during the night. The fire chief pulled a hose toward the house, its roof now completely ablaze.

"My word," said Bud in shock when he saw.

Truman scanned the gathering crowd and spotted Jenny in her nightgown holding Queenie, her face dark with soot, her hair shooting out in all directions. She was staring into the flames, tears streaming down her cheeks, leaving trails on her ash-covered face.

Sook lay on her back, out of breath, her white hair fanned across the grass. As Truman wiped her face, she stared into his eyes and felt his cheek with her hand.

"It's really *is* you, isn't it?"

He nodded.

"You came home for Christmas . . ." Her gaze drifted to the house. "Oh, dear—the house is on fire."

Bud tried to clear his throat. He was having trouble getting a good breath.

"Are you—"

"I'll be fine, Little Chappie," he said, hacking.

Truman felt someone to his left and he looked up to see Jenny standing over him. "Truman?" she asked, her voice coarse from the smoke.

He smiled and she fell to her knees and grabbed him. He had never seen her cry before, for she was the always-tough-as-nails boss of everyone. But he could feel the warm tears fall on his neck.

The house was soon consumed by flames, a giant bonfire that reached fifty feet into the air, billows of black smoke blocking out the stars. The hydrant was useless, as it had rusted shut. Neighbors came out of their houses in their nightclothes, armed with shovels and buckets, to keep the fire from spreading to their own homes. The fire bellowed like a wounded dragon, wood popping and crackling, interrupted by exploding windows that shot smoke and flames into the night air.

"Poor Callie. Now there's nothing left of her," said Jenny to no one.

Truman watched as the entire roof collapsed in a matter of minutes, and just like that, the house that Truman had spent his childhood in was gone.

Everyone gazed into the flames, lost in thought. The blistering heat from the fire had melted all the frost in the yard. A few neighbors came over bearing blankets; they lifted Sook and Bud off the wet ground and wrapped them up.

Truman heard chattering and realized it was his teeth from the wintry chill.

"Come on, you'll catch your death out here," Jenny said.

Truman, Sook, Jenny, Bud, and Queenie were led around the side of the house, where they could see the street filled with people, some carrying buckets of water, others shoveling dirt onto the glowing carcass of their former house.

Blind Captain Wash, who lived across the street with his crippled wife, was having a row about being made to leave his home in the middle of the night. He was wearing nothing but a nightshirt and a Rebel cap.

On his way through the crowd, Truman tripped and fell to the ground. When he looked up, he saw his mysterious neighbor, Sonny Boular, standing over him.

At least, that's who he thought it was. The lights from the flames danced and when he scrambled to his feet, Sonny was nowhere to be seen. Truman's eyes must have been playing tricks on him.

As the winds turned, the firemen seemed to have given up on saving the house and focused instead on saving the nearby homes from catching fire. Including the Lee household.

"Nelle," said Truman. He moved toward her house, pushing his way through the crowd. He heard piano music in the distance and suddenly ran right into Mr. Lee, who was gazing at the fire.

"I shouldn't have burned that dogwood. Too many flying embers . . ."

Truman tugged on his sleeve. "Mr. Lee, Mr. Lee. Where's Nelle?"

Mr. Lee seemed lost in a haze. Then the piano music started again and they saw Mrs. Lee in her robe pushing the piano to an open window.

He and Truman went over to find Nelle's two older sisters, Bear and Weezie, trying to pull their mother away from the piano. Weezie was always prim and proper, which was difficult to manage under the circumstances. Mrs. Lee was easily excitable and prone to playing piano at two in the morning, much to the consternation of her neighbors.

"Mother. Come on, we need to leave," said Bear sternly.

"But I haven't finished," she said as she sat down to play again.

Nelle wasn't there. Truman noticed her brother, whom they just called Brother, as he was the only one, pumping water into a bucket from an outdoor pump. Truman ran over.

"Have you seen Nelle?"

Brother was too busy dousing the house to get into a conversation. "She's out here somewhere!" he said, and moved on.

Truman's eyes darted from the crowd to the house and back again. No Nelle. He scanned the property along the horse-bone fence, by the double chinaberry tree, and up to the treehouse.

He noticed that someone crawling in. "Nelle," he said to himself.

He also noticed that some of the branches of the tree were on fire.

8

All Things Must Pass

Truman scrambled up the ladder to the treehouse like a squirrel in heat. When he burst through the trapdoor, he came face to face with Nelle, her arms full of books.

"I saw you were okay," she said. "Are you? Everybody made it out?"

Truman had to catch his breath. "What are you doing?"

"Thought I'd save a few things . . ." she said, although everything was old and dusty and mostly useless anyway. "Just for old times' sake."

Truman stared at her. "You do know the tree's on fire?"

"Why do you think I'm here?" she said. "We can't let books burn."

"None of this junk matters anymore . . ." said Truman, his voice trailing off.

She felt bad for him. "Oh, Tru. I'm sorry. You came all this way, and now . . ."

Truman frowned as he watched the flicker of the light dance off her face. "I guess I'm still cursed," he mumbled.

She knew what he meant. "You and me both," she said.

They flinched when a branch broke off and fell with a thump onto the roof. "Come on, we best get out before we're toast," said Truman.

Nelle nodded. "Take these." She dumped the books into his arms and turned to grab some more. Truman dangled his legs down the trapdoor. "How'm I supposed to climb with my arms full?"

"Just drop 'em!" she said. She tossed some more books his way, so he started dropping them through the hatch and watching them plummet to the ground.

She filled her pockets with knickknacks, grabbing whatever she could.

"We have to go," said Truman.

Nelle took a long look around. "Hold on . . ."

Truman could see the leaves around the fort catching fire. "Now."

"I just want to remember it," she said. "Remember all the books we read and stories we wrote?"

He did, of course. Reading and writing were the only things that kept him going. "We can still do it. Just not here."

She nodded.

"One other thing," said Truman. "I . . . ran away. No one knows why I'm here yet except you."

She studied his face and smiled. "I already figured. I can tell when you're fibbing. Your ears turn pink."

He smiled. It was time to go. Even though their hearts were beating a mile a minute, they paused and took it all in, knowing it was the last time they'd see their old headquarters.

Then, without a word, they descended back to earth.

On the ground, they both looked up at their fort as it caught fire.

"Don't that beat all," Nelle muttered.

They watched it burn together.

9

The Morning After

By morning, there was nothing left except the blackened remains of Jenny's house and a frozen fireman's jacket standing up straight like a ghost on what used to be the front porch.

The treehouse was gone. But luckily, the wind had died down during the night and Nelle's house was spared. Nelle's mother was finally asleep after hours of hysterics. Jenny, Sook, and Bud sat on Nelle's side porch in a daze, trying to figure out what had happened.

Everything Truman had come back for had gone up in smoke. The house he grew up in, gone. His beloved treehouse, gone. Nothing would ever be the same.

"I'll rebuild," said Jenny. "I don't care what it takes, I won't let a fire turn us out onto the streets."

A.C. was not his normal self. He was black with soot from fighting the fire all night and sat staring at the charred husk, shaking his head. "It's all my fault. I should have known better . . ."

"Hush, Mr. Lee," said Jenny. "I won't have it."

"But it was my fault, don't you see? The embers . . ." he said, looking up at his chimney. "Any fool could see which way the wind was blowing . . ."

Jenny put her hand on his shoulder. "Fact is, the fire marshal warned me a year ago to clean all the leaves off my roof. I was stingy, didn't want to pay someone to go up there. You couldn't have known."

A.C. put his hand on hers and looked her in the eye. "I want you to know that I will do whatever I can to help you rebuild— even if I have to do it myself."

Jenny grimaced. "I know it, Mr. Lee. But I am not a charity case. My father built this home and I will rebuild it myself."

He considered her words and knew she was determined. "Then you all will stay with us while you rebuild. That way you can be close. I insist."

"I thank you. But I don't think, with Mrs. Lee and all . . ."

A.C. rubbed his wedding ring and noticed that it was scratched. "Hmm."

"Don't you worry about us, A.C. We've been through scrapes

before, and considering what people have gone through these past few years, I'm grateful we haven't ended up in Mudtown. We'll manage somehow . . ."

Sook held a miniature Bible that she'd found to her chest and asked God to guide them through the day. Truman and Nelle sifted through the scorched wreckage with a stick. When they found something half singed, they held it up for Jenny or Bud to decide whether they wanted to keep it. In addition to the Bible, they'd recovered a rolling pin, a smoked ham, a bottle of whiskey, and, best of all, a small scrapbook of family photos.

Nelle was flipping through the scrapbook and saw a picture of Truman standing in a creek. "Remember when you used to catch catfish with your bare hands? You used to dam up the little river and pick them up to pet them like kittens. You still do that?"

"You can't do that in New York," said Truman. "In fact, you can't do anything up there that you do down here. Being from the South up there is like being a two-headed calf. You're a freak show. And considering I'm already a freak . . ."

"That's nonsense," said Nelle. "You shouldn't say such things." Just then, she came across a picture of them when he was seven. He was wearing his little white suit. She was in her overalls. She laughed. "Remember when I asked you to marry me? Under the yellow rosebushes over there? And you said you'd think about it?"

Truman blushed but didn't say anything.

"And then you came back and said okay, but I'd changed my mind?" she said. "Boy, were you snooty after that."

"I didn't care one way or the other. I was seven," he said.

"You ran away with that Martha girl to make me jealous," she added.

"Did not," he said. "I was just lighting out for the territories, is all. And Martha came along for the ride."

"Did you kiss her?"

Truman blushed even deeper. "Never you mind. But no. Maybe I kissed someone else."

Nelle's eyes lit up. "Who? Mabel?"

Truman made a face and focused back on digging through the rubble. "Maybe it was a boy," he said quietly.

Nelle's jaw dropped. Truman ignored her. Then she thought twice and laughed. "*Right.* That's a good one."

Truman bent down to pick up a charred cookie tin. He struggled but managed to pry it open. Inside was a pile of pictures Sook had cut out from glamour magazines. "Oh, look!" he said. "Sook's movie queens."

Nelle went over to have a look. She propped her head on his shoulder. As Truman flipped though the Hollywood starlets, he made little fawning sounds. "Aww, isn't she lovely . . ."

She could feel that her presence made him nervous. "How come you never kissed me?"

Truman stopped flipping. "Because you're my friend," he said quietly.

"So?" she said.

He shrugged. "It's like kissing your sister."

"Oh—so I'm like a sister now?" She was teasing.

Truman grew flustered. "No, I didn't mean that." He dropped the photos and began to stutter. "It's just, it—it's just . . ."

Nelle came around to face him. They were standing behind the remains of the chimney, out of view of the others. Suddenly, she realized how tired and sad and pained he was. "I'm sorry, Tru, I was just messing—"

He leaned in and kissed her.

It was not like the movies.

They both pulled back, red-faced, and realized how wrong it felt. But it was not like kissing a sibling.

"Sorry," he said awkwardly.

She shook her head. "That's okay. I know I'm not a boy . . ."

He tilted his head and studied her. She grinned shyly.

Right then, a flatbed truck came rumbling down the road, honking its blustery horn and making a mighty ruckus. Truman and Nelle stared as the truck skidded to a halt near them.

Out popped Big Boy's mother and father, Mary Ida and Jennings Sr., a plainspoken couple who farmed and loved riding around on a motorcycle with a sidecar.

"Ohmygoodnessohmygoodness—" Mary Ida said, rushing up to Jenny. She was tiny but solid—a force of nature when she needed to be. "We just heard. You poor darling. Your poor house!" She hugged Jenny, who was too tired to care.

Jennings Sr. was tall and tanned and usually smiling, but not this time. He shook hands with Bud and spoke in hushed tones, with a look of grave concern etched on his face.

The Morning After

When Truman looked back at the truck, Big Boy was standing there gaping—not at the burnt ruins, but at Truman. Big Boy had a peculiar expression on his face, as if he wasn't sure if he was seeing a ghost.

He slowly walked up to where Truman stood, and when he was three feet away, he tilted his head, trying to make sense of it.

"Don't worry, he ain't a ghost, it's really him," Nelle said to Big Boy.

Big Boy reached out with his finger and poked Truman.

"Hiya, Big Boy," said Truman.

Big Boy flinched, then giggled, staring in wonderment. "What happened to you?" he asked.

Truman looked to Nelle for interpretation. "I'm here too, Big Boy," she said in response.

He ignored her. "Why are you . . ."

"Here?" asked Truman.

"Dressed like . . ."

"A soldier?"

Big Boy took in Truman's uniform, now soiled and ruined. It looked like he'd just survived the Battle of Monroeville. Then he happened to glance up and see the burnt treehouse. "Oh no . . ." Then the charred house, as if he'd somehow missed it before. "Oh no!"

Big Boy stood there gawking at the mess. "I'm so sorry . . . We just heard or we woulda come last night. Nobody said you were here."

"Well, I am," said Truman.

Big Boy was at a loss for words. "How are you?" he finally asked.

Truman sighed. "Cursed."

Big Boy nodded as if that meant something. "You look . . . different." Then: "Did you join up?" he asked.

Nelle interjected, "He ran away from military school."

Big Boy ignored her, waiting for Truman to reply.

"I'm AWOL," said Truman. "Don't tell the others."

"Oh," said Big Boy. "What's *a wall*?"

"AWOL," said Nelle, rolling her eyes. "It means he's absent without leave. Right?"

"It means I left without permission," said Truman.

"Oh." Big Boy nodded, still ignoring Nelle. "Why were you in military school? What does your mom think about you being here?"

"It's a long story. And she doesn't know I'm here," he said quietly. "She and Joe are in Cuba visiting Joe's family. But she'll find out sooner or later. I don't know what I'm gonna do now. I was looking forward to having a nice Christmas, just like we used to . . ."

"You can stay with us," said Big Boy and Nelle at the same time.

They glared at each other.

"It's settled, then," announced Jennings Sr. from the porch. "You're all staying with us till you get back on your feet."

Big Boy stuck his tongue out at Nelle.

"What are you, four?" said Nelle.

Jenny was taken aback. "But . . . you couldn't possibly house all of us—"

Jennings surveyed the group. "Of course we can. We got plenty of room on the farm. We'll just have to improvise—is that young Truman?"

Mary Ida looked up and grinned. She walked over and hugged him like a long-lost soul. "My, what a Christmas present you make. Lillie Mae's not here, is she?"

"No, ma'am," said Truman. "She and Joe went to Cuba to see family."

"And they didn't take you? Their loss is my gain."

"Jennings," said Jenny, "I cannot accept your kind and generous offer."

Mary Ida brushed aside her objections. "You can and will. And I'll hear no more about it! We're family," said Mary Ida. "And family sticks together. Isn't that right, Dad?"

"You heard her." Jennings Sr. nodded. "'Sides, I got me an extra-big hog for Christmas dinner. How'm I gonna eat it all by myself—"

There was a loud scream and everyone turned to the burned ruins, where Little Bit stood staring at the remains of her oven, Ol' Buckeye. "My kitchen! *What happened to my kitchen?*"

"Better make room for one more," said Sook. "I cain't cook Christmas supper without Lil' Bit."

10
Cramped Quarters

ig Boy lived on a farm out on Drewry Road, a mile or so from the center of town. It was a simple plot of land that normally grew corn and cotton and had a small herd of milking cows and a few pigs. It was surrounded by deep woods and muddy roads and usually smelled of honeysuckle and cow dung. Now it was just cold and barren except for some winter crops struggling to take hold.

Mary Ida stood on her front porch as Truman's family glumly marched into the farmhouse with nothing but the clothes on their backs, the blankets they'd been given, and whatever belongings that could be saved, which weren't much. She was used to taking in stray animals and nursing them back to health. She had once found a dying vulture and brought it back from the dead, even taught it to fly again. But weariness was catching up to this group of strays. Not even a welcoming table of biscuits and molasses and banana pudding could raise their mood.

"We'll get you new clothes as soon as we can," said Mary Ida. "Some of your neighbors are going through their closets and gathering whatever clothes they can spare. But for now, let's get you out of these and into a bath as soon as Bama gets that water hot."

"Yes'm," said Bama, their ornery cook. She stared sourly at the soot and dirt they were tracking in. "Might be easier if everyone just jumped in the river."

"Bama, that river is like an arctic bath. If it gets any colder, we'll be able to go ice skating on it," said Mary Ida.

"Yes'm," said Bama. "I ain't never seen that river froze since I was a pup. Something in the air this season. I just hope it don't snow. Ruin them crops fer sure."

Jennings Sr. helped Sook ease into a rocking chair and gave her a dab of her favorite Brown's Mule tobacco chaw to calm her nerves. As she rocked back and forth, dabbing her mouth with an old handkerchief, Truman noticed how frail she'd become. Same with Bud and Jenny. It the raw light of the winter morning, he realized his family was old.

"Truman," said Mary Ida, "you can sleep with Big Boy."

Tru smiled. He'd never had any siblings to play with growing up. Maybe this would turn out to be a good thing.

"We are gonna have so much fun, Truman! I don't know why you didn't stay with us before—it'll be like sleepovers but, you know, longer."

"There's work to do, boys," said Jennings Sr. "After you're cleaned and rested, maybe Truman can help Big Boy tend to the winter crops. They need covering before the freeze sets in."

Big Boy laughed. "Truman work the fields? That'll be the day . . ."

Truman made a face. "Maybe I can husk the corn and shell the peas or feed the chickens," he said.

Jennings Sr. put his hand on Truman's shoulder. "That's women's work, son. You're starting to fill out some. And you look fine in that uniform, ready for battle." He wiped some soot off his hand.

"I'll do what I can, sir," said Truman, much to Big Boy's amazement.

"Thank you, son. Gone are the days where you'd just sit here and gaze at the flowers. Bet that school beat the sissy right out of you, right, son?"

Truman blanched. Mary Ida swatted Jennings with her hand. "Dad, don't be picking on poor Truman. He's a delicate soul. If he wants to stare at flowers all day, let him." She gave Tru a hug.

There was something about Big Boy and his family that Truman had always liked. Unlike everyone else in his extended family, they seemed almost normal.

Still, they all stood around in a state of shock, as if they'd just come in from the front lines. Mary Ida called out room assignments. "Sook can sleep with me. Bud and Jennings Sr. can take the front room. Jenny can set up in the sunroom. Little Bit, you go in the kitchen and help Bama get supper going."

No one seemed happy, but what choice did they have? They were soggy and tired and sneezing from the chill. Mary Ida felt for them and knew she had to take charge. "Well?" she said when no one stirred. "Get moving!"

Jenny had to swallow her pride as the matriarch of the family. Her frosty blue eyes seemed somewhat dimmed, and her hair, usually the crowning glory of her regal appearance, looked colorless and unkempt. But she was nothing if not resilient and had saved her family from ruin and poverty before. "I thank you for taking us in. But we'll stay only until the new house gets walls. I've already talked to Mr. Horton about rebuilding. He said he'll start on it as soon as he can."

Jennings Sr. shook his head. "Not till the spring thaw, I reckon. Ain't nobody gonna build nothing in these conditions. Almanac says we're in for the coldest winter in fifty years."

Jenny knew he was right, but she had to add, "I won't let a fire get the best of me, and I sure won't let a little frost stop me either." She was used to getting her way.

Most of them eyed their new roommates with trepidation or surliness or both. Big Boy, however, was beside himself at the idea that Truman would stay in his room. "I'm sorry for the fire, but sometimes there's a silver lining. This is gonna be swell, having you stay here," he said without thinking.

Little Bit and Bama were having a showdown at the kitchen door. They knew each other from way back when they were kids and were always fighting over whatever meager toy they might have. "You best git out the way, Bama, if you know what's good for you. Who knows, maybe you'll even learn a thing or two from watching me—like how to *cook*."

Bama stared Little Bit down hard. "You a little bit o' trouble, as far as I reckon. You think I'm gonna let you in *my* kitchen? Ha, you dumber than you look!"

Sook intervened. "'Scuse me, girls. I'm gonna git supper ready, if'n you don't mind." She stepped in and got the lay of the land. She wasn't happy. "No. This won't do. Let's move this table over here, and these chairs here—" Even though she was well into her sixties, she had no trouble moving things about. "And this here . . ."

Bama glared at Little Bit, who shrugged. "She like that. But you can keep her under control, *if'n* you know how . . ."

Bama scowled, then took a step back to let her pass. But as Little Bit walked by, Bama grabbed her arm. "Just remember whose kitchen this is, missy."

Little Bit removed Bama's hand from her arm and pointed to the scar that ran from her eye to her chin. "See this here scar? Had another woman going after my man and she done this to me." She glanced back at the kitchen. "She ain't around no more to show you hers . . ."

"Girls!" said Sook. "There's only four days till Christmas.

And so much to do. Heaven knows how we'll manage, but we'll make do. Now let's get to work!"

"Come and get it!" Truman yelled as he banged on the metal triangle Mary Ida had hanging on her front porch. She grinned behind him, knowing how much he had loved doing that when he was smaller.

Midday supper was the main meal of the day. Mary Ida had a table big enough to feed an army, but even that wasn't big enough for this group once some of the sharecroppers came in from the cold. All of them would have to spread out and sit where they could.

Included in the group of workers was the father of their black friend Edison, a man everyone called Cousin. Truman kept an eye out for Edison, whose imitations of things like trains and planes entertained everyone. But his pa said Edison was working on some mystery project and couldn't be bothered with things like eating.

When the food appeared, Truman realized he hadn't had a warm meal in days, and the smell of his favorite butter beans made his mouth water. As soon as Little Bit put the bowl in front of him, he started wolfing them down.

"Truman! Mind your manners. Wait until everyone has some," said Jenny.

"Oh, let the boy have his butter beans. Can't you see he's starving?" said Bud.

Truman swallowed and felt the warmth grow in his stomach. "Sorry, Jenny. It's just that they're so *gooood*."

Bama and Mary Ida brought in the main dishes. "Fried squirrel!" said Bud. "What happened to that ham you been bragging about, Jennings?"

Jennings Sr. shrugged. "Squirrels is what we got these days. Feeding pigs is too expensive. Saving my one hog for Christmas Day, Bud. Then we'll have us a feast!"

In came the corn bread and honey in the comb, black-eyed peas, wild asparagus, and corn. And even though it was getting too cold to fish, Cousin had managed to catch two catfish and had had Bama fry them up. For the moment, all seemed right with the world, even though everything else was wrong.

"How's that writing coming, Mr. Truman?" asked Cousin.

Truman was chewing on a bit of squirrel. "Haven't done much lately," he said. "I got in trouble because I turned in a story at school that was so good, none of the teachers believed that I wrote it."

Cousin chuckled. "You do have a way with words, Mr. Truman."

"I remember the time you wrote that story for the Sunshine Page called 'Ol' Mrs. Busybody,'" said Jenny. "Everyone in the neighborhood thought you were writing about them. Especially Mrs. Lee. Truman caused quite a scandal as an eight-year-old. I made him apologize to everyone on the block."

"Well, he's a born writer, I'll tell you that much," said Bud.

"Tried his hand at tap dancing until we wanted to kill him 'cause he made such a racket. But he was always carrying around one of those Red Chief tablets and writing things down."

"Tell us a story, Mr. Truman. Help raise everyone's spirits just a little," said Cousin.

Truman frowned, put down his fork. "I'm not really in the mood," he said.

"Come on, Tru, it'll make you feel better," said Sook.

He thought for a moment. "When we first moved to New York, I told Nina—Lillie Mae—that I wanted to visit the famous Bronx Zoo. Well, she was too busy and had no interest in seeing a bunch of smelly animals, so she had the nanny take me."

"You have a nanny?" asked Big Boy.

"*Had*. She was a large woman named Helga who was fresh off the boat from Sweden and was terrified of tigers and lions. But Lillie Mae made her take me to the zoo, and wouldn't you know, there we were, having a grand old time looking at monkeys and zebras, when suddenly pandemonium broke out!"

"What happened?" asked Bud.

"Well, I'll tell you. Men and women and children were screaming and running for their lives. A lion had escaped its cage and was headed our way! Helga panicked and ran faster than a cheetah chasing a gazelle. Left me all alone with that bloodthirsty animal on the prowl."

"What'd you do?" asked Big Boy.

Truman sighed. "I don't know what came over me. I froze

when I saw the great beast coming down the path for me. My only thought was how much it'd hurt to be swallowed whole by a giant cat. I—"

"Wait a minute," interrupted Jennings Sr. "Is this the one where it comes right up to you and you start singing 'You Are My Sunshine' till it rolls over on its belly and purrs?"

Truman stared at his plate, the wind taken out of his sails.

"Dad!" said Mary Ida as she slapped his hand. "Let him tell his story."

"No, that's okay," said Truman glumly. "That was how it ended."

There was a long, awkward pause till Cousin spoke. "I hate lions. I get all heebie-jeebie whenever I see one."

"When did you ever see a lion?" asked Bud.

As Cousin started recounting a tale about a wildcat that kept eating his chickens, the focus drifted away from Truman. Even his gift for gab was abandoning him.

11
A Vision

S now. Truman stood in a forest watching snowflakes drop silently from the gray skies. He opened his mouth, giddy, and let the snowflakes melt on his tongue. He couldn't taste anything.

Tru noticed the flakes falling on his freshly pressed uniform. He was standing in a foot of snow but didn't feel cold for some reason. But when he looked up, he saw it: the perfect Christmas tree.

Even though he was in the middle of a forest, the tree stood apart from the others. It was decorated with popcorn strings, ornaments, and candles. He'd never seen anything so beautiful.

Next thing he knew, the tree was in a house. It was not Jenny's house or Mary Ida's but a new one. He could smell the newness of the wood floors. Sook was there serving fruitcake, Bud was smoking a pipe and tending to the fire, Jenny was smiling as she opened a present. Big Boy and Nelle sat on the floor with Truman, drinking hot apple cider. He found a small envelope with his name on it and opened it. Inside was a piece of paper. He pulled it out and read it. All it said was *Cursed*.

When he looked up again, the tree was gone; the presents were gone. Sook, Jenny, and Bud, gone. Big Boy and Nelle were walking away.

"Wait!" he cried out. "Don't leave me!"

"I'm not going anywhere," said Big Boy.

Truman blinked. He was sitting up in bed in Big Boy's room. Big Boy was sitting on the floor cleaning his air rifle.

"You were talking in your sleep," said Big Boy. "Thought you might go sleepwalking like in the old days."

Truman plopped back into his pillow. "I must've been dreaming. Give me something to write on, quick!"

Big Boy searched through his school bag and found a composition book. "I need that back," he said, handing it over.

"I've been keeping a dream book where I write down all my dreams before I forget them."

"Why do you do that?" asked Big Boy.

"So I can free up my brain for thinking," he said.

"I dream of flyin'," said Big Boy. "Ever since Pa let me fly with that barnstormer during the Hog Fest. When I grow up, I wanna be a crop-duster."

"A crop-duster is a plane, not a person," said Truman as he wrote. "You mean a crop-duster pilot."

"That's what I said."

"Never mind," said Truman as he finished up his dream writing. "Say, when do you usually get your Christmas tree?"

"Pa likes to go out on Christmas Eve and chop one down."

Truman sat up. "I know a good one. Maybe you and me could go get it before someone else does," he said.

"You mean today? It's already midafternoon. We're supposed to help cover crops."

Truman rubbed his eyes. "I must've really conked out. But really, we have to go get it. It's a big one too. Best tree I ever saw. Might need to get Nelle to help us."

Big Boy stopped cleaning the air rifle. "We can manage."

Truman swung his legs over the side of the bed. "Say, what's with you two? You didn't even talk to her."

He frowned. "I don't know. Lately, she's been acting all different. She gets all weird and stuff around me too. I don't like it. She's not like she used to be."

"How do you mean?"

Big Boy hemmed and hawed. "She's—you know . . ."

"What?" Truman asked, concerned.

Big Boy sighed. "A girl. Okay?"

Truman started laughing. "Well, of course she's a girl!"

Big Boy blushed. "You and me both know Nelle Lee was never no girl."

"So you don't talk to her because . . . she's a *girl?*"

"It's not just that," he said carefully. "I think . . . she *likes* me. You know, like *that.*"

Truman just stared at him. "I'm pretty sure she doesn't like you like *that.*"

"How do you know?"

Truman thought about telling him about the kiss. "I just do. Now, can we go get this tree?"

Big Boy looked out the window. Jennings Sr. was outside trying to get the pump unstuck from the frost. "Why you so intent on this tree?"

"I told you, I'm cursed."

Big Boy scrunched up his face. "Well, what does a tree have to do with that?"

Truman got up and put on some of Big Boy's old clothes. "It's hard to explain. We never had a Christmas tree when I was little. We were either on the road or didn't have the money. And when I was living at Jenny's, we always had a puny tree because Jenny thought it was a waste of a good tree to cut it down for just a few days of pageantry. But in the movies, you see those perfect Christmases and everything is just right, and the family comes together and everyone is happy and all their problems get solved—and it's all because they have a perfect tree."

Big Boy didn't see the logic. "I don't know. One's as good as the next," he said, getting to his feet and stretching.

"But I saw it. It was like a vision. It was—"

Suddenly, through the window, Big Boy spotted someone in

the distance walking their way. It looked like Nelle. "Okay, then let's go."

"Really?"

"What are you waiting for? We'll go get Edison and chop that tree down and get it back here by sundown."

Big Boy was already headed out the door before Truman could get his boots on. Truman caught a glimpse of himself in the mirror: overalls, plaid shirt, boots, and coat. He looked just like Big Boy.

12
A Turn of Events

Big Boy bundled up, grabbed his ax, and headed out to the fields. He didn't stop to talk to his ma, knowing she'd think they were headed out to cover the crops. Truman ran to catch up.

"Where you going?" Truman called out.

Big Boy pointed into the icy wind to a small shed way on the other end of the field. "To find Edison, of course." Edison was a black kid who other boys always made fun of because his head seemed smaller than it should be and he was slow to catch on to things. But he had a big heart, loved to imitate sounds, and would do anything to help out.

Truman caught up to Big Boy. His face was already pink from the cold. "He lives out here?"

"When Cousin started working for us, my pa let him build this shed to live in. Pa likes them close. He plays checkers with Cousin or Edison whenever he can."

"Bud's like that too. He plays cards with his field hand more than he makes him work," said Truman.

"Look. There he is," said Big Boy. "Don't mention his stutter. He's been doing it since summer."

Truman saw someone digging a hole in the ground. He was about waist deep and making sounds like a steam shovel excavating the earth. "What's he doing? Digging a grave?"

"Don't ask. And don't mention the pool either. You'll never hear the end of it," said Big Boy.

"The pool? In this weather" asked Truman, slapping his arms for warmth. Edison stopped digging and turned to see them coming.

"*Shh.* I told you don't mention it," hissed Big Boy. He smiled and waved at Edison. "Heya, look who come to visit!"

Edison let out a pneumatic *hisssss* sound and put his shovel down, squinting at Truman. It took Edison a few seconds, but then a big grin broke out on his face. "T-Troooman? Is that *y-you?*"

"It is I," Truman said elegantly, and took a bow.

Edison climbed out of his hole and ran over to see him. He went in for a hug and practically choked the life out of him. "I m-missed you," he said.

"Really? Um . . . thanks," said Truman.

Big Boy stood there watching and then, feeling jealous, stepped in for a hug too.

Edison broke away. "Sook gave me your old p-plane. Look!" He pointed to a lone tree in the open field, where the plane sat nestled in its branches.

"Oh . . . nice," said Truman. "So what're you doing, digging a hole to China?"

Edison stopped smiling and stared into the dirt.

"Oh, come on, Edison," said Big Boy. "He didn't mean nothing by it."

Truman looked at Big Boy, confused. Big Boy gestured for him not to worry about it. "Um, hey, Edison, you want to come with us? We're on a mission."

"Where you g-going?" asked Edison.

"We're gonna destroy Truman's curse by cutting down a Christmas tree. We need your help," said Big Boy.

"C-curse?" asked Edison. "Maybe Lil' B-Bit can do s-something fer you. She's a v-voodoo queen, you know."

"It's complicated," said Truman, not wanting to explain. "Would you like to come or not?"

Edison didn't even question it. He grabbed his shovel. "Yes, s-sir," he said.

"Don't do that, Edison. It's just me and Truman," said Big Boy.

Edison nodded and smiled like an eager puppy. "Yes . . . friends!"

The trio wandered for half an hour through the forest. "It's kind of like the boys' club all over again, ain't it?" asked Big Boy.

"'Cept Nelle isn't here," said Truman.

A Turn of Events

"Well, she ain't a— Oh, never mind. Just where the heck is this tree of yours?" asked Big Boy.

Truman looked around to get his bearings. He was lost. And the only sound he could hear was the creaking of the aspen trees as they swayed in the wind.

Fifteen minutes later, Truman was perched high up in one of those aspens, looking for his special tree and hoping the red belt he'd left behind would pop out among all the browns and greens.

When Truman was a child, he and Sook would climb to the top of the trees that surrounded Big Boy's farm and hang on tight as the blustery winds of winter tried to blow them off. It was a game they played, but more important, from that high up, they could spot the best Christmas trees. Sook would tuck her dress into her drawers, and up the slender white trunks they'd climb, one each, high enough that the trees wobbled and wavered. They'd hold on, surveying the land and listening to the murmur of the aspens as they swayed in the gusts.

"This tree *is* in Alabama, ain't it? We musta passed a hundred great trees by now!" shouted Big Boy.

"They're not the ones," said Truman, holding on for dear life. "Besides, I think we're close now."

Truman squinted into the arctic winds as the branches slapped at his face, threatening to break his hold. He thought he saw something red up ahead, but it was hard to tell because he was getting seasick. "I'm coming down."

When Truman was earthbound again, he pointed north. "I think we should go that way."

Edison was shivering. "I'm c-cold."

"Well, you shoulda worn your coat," said Big Boy. "Just think of a big Christmas feast and that'll warm you up some."

Edison looked puzzled. "C-Christmas don't hold much for us. We don't got no money for f-feasts."

"Yes, but the Christmas spirit is free, isn't it?" asked Truman. "I'll pick out a little tree for you. I've a good eye for such things."

Edison's face scrunched up. "How's a t-tree gonna kill your c-curse, again?" he asked.

Truman kept walking. "I don't know, Edison, but it will. I can feel it."

Big Boy sidled up to Truman and whispered, "Don't get him a tree. They don't have room in that shack of theirs." He turned to Edison. "Hey, Edison, you all can come over for Christmas at our house if you like."

Edison stopped. "You saying . . . we invited over for *C-Christmas?*"

Big Boy looked at Truman. Truman shrugged. "Why not? We already got a full house. Two more won't hurt."

Edison stared at his feet. "What's wrong?" asked Big Boy.

"Nobody n-never invited us over for C-Christmas before," he said quietly. "'Specially no w-white folks."

"Well, we ain't white folk. We're family. I don't see any difference except you're a bit darker, is all," said Big Boy. "'Sides,

94

you're a full-fledged member of the Drewry Road Boys' Club, ain't ya?"

Edison's eyes lit up. "R-really?" he asked.

"Heck yeah," said Big Boy. "Of course you're part of it."

Edison stood up proud. "If'n you say so."

"He does, and so do I," said Truman. "Why, in New York, we have colored people over all the time. It's not like down here."

Edison grew misty-eyed. "I don't believe you're c-cursed, Mr. Truman. Nothing c-cursed could make me feel so . . . good."

Big Boy slapped Truman on the back. "See? Now let's go find you your tree. That's a fine thing to do among friends."

Ten minutes later, they were staring at Truman's red cadet belt. It was wrapped around a tree trunk.

Only there wasn't a tree attached to it.

"Where your t-tree at?" asked Edison.

Truman grew red in the face. "I knew it. I knew it was too good to be true."

"Now, hold on there, Tru. It ain't worth crying over," said Big Boy. "It's just a tree." He scanned the forest. "Why, we could take that tree over there! That would look great by the fireplace."

But Truman wasn't having it. "Someone stole my tree."

"Well, officially, it wasn't exactly yours. God put it there first," said Big Boy.

"For me to find!" Truman shook his head. "I claimed it. That makes it mine. It's all because I'm cursed, don't you see? They could have taken any of these trees, but they took mine. What are the odds?" He plopped down on the frigid brown earth and stared at the stump. "I don't understand why everything always gets taken from me."

"Don't be silly, Truman," said Big Boy. "It's just a run of bad luck. It happens. And it's usually followed by a run of good luck. So that's it! I now declare this bad-luck thing over. Forget the tree. Let the good luck begin, starting . . . *now!*"

"No," said Edison. "I know what you sayin', T-Truman. 'Member that time you d-done saved me from d-drowning? I made fun of Bama's c-cooking that morning and she done c-cursed me. And this past summer, with the p-pool? I done it again. We got to break that c-curse before it get a hold of you fer g-good."

Normally Truman would've laughed at such a statement. But he really felt cursed. He felt it in his bones, like his mother had cursed him the day he was born into this world.

"What should we do?" he asked.

Big Boy threw up his hands and groaned. "Aww, heck . . . you can't be serious."

"We got to get that t-tree back," said Edison. "S-stop the bad luck. Or else it'll stop y-you."

"Just how in the heck we gonna to do that?" said Big Boy.

Edison pointed to the dirt. Whoever cut down the tree had dragged it off, leaving a trail.

13

Tree Trackers

The culprit had to be big enough to have carried the tree by himself. The footsteps were deep, and when Truman stuck his foot in one, his foot was half its size.

"I heard about this creature they call Bigfoot, but I thought that was out west," said Truman.

"Well, this one's wearing boots," said Big Boy. "And I ain't keen on tangling with it for a measly tree."

Truman glanced over at Big Boy, disappointed. "Look here, I had to escape military school with nothing but the clothes on my back, then hop on a freight train filled with hoboes only to see my house burn down. And, well, if you're too scared, Edison and I will be more than happy to do battle on our own, won't we?"

Edison didn't answer because he was staring at the foot-prints too.

"Come on, Big Boy. Have I ever steered you wrong?" said Truman.

He had, plenty. But it generally worked out in the end. "Aww, Tru. You always manage to talk me into things," said Big Boy.

"That's because you're my friend," he said.

"Yeah, but I always end up regrettin' it later," said Big Boy.

They followed the path through the forest and up a hill. They were panting by the time they reached the top.

Big Boy caught his breath. "So . . . what're we gonna do when we find the guy who did this? Beat him up? Steal your tree back?"

"We'll figure it out when we find him," Truman answered. "Besides, no one's going to tangle with your ax and Edison's shovel."

"That's t-true," said Edison. "At least, I h-hope so."

They came over the top of the hill and gazed down at Mudtown, the shantytown on the outskirts of Monroeville where the poor, the destitute, and the dregs of society ended up. Mudtown represented the bottom of the barrel, and by the fourth year of the Great Depression, it had tripled in size.

"The trail goes down there," said Truman.

They all looked down at the mass of "buildings"—homes made of scrap wood, cardboard, tarps, and the like. Even though it was freezing, they could see women cooking over outdoor fires, huddled in blankets, some even with bare feet.

"I ain't going in there," said Big Boy. "Probably some poor sap just burning it to keep warm."

"No," said Edison. "L-look!"

He pointed to a gulley that surrounded the shantytown, where there was a lone figure dragging the tree up an embankment.

A big figure.

At first, Truman didn't recognize him, but his sheer size left no doubt.

"Boss Henderson," said Truman. A chill ran down his spine, and suddenly, even he had doubts.

Boss. The biggest, meanest bully in Monroe County. Even though he was only fourteen, adults didn't mess with him.

"Boss . . ." Edison gritted his teeth and hoisted his shovel up onto his shoulder. "Let's go get that t-tree."

"Take it easy, Edison." Truman patted his back. "We should think this through."

"The only thing to think is whether he'll eat us all and still have room for dessert," said Big Boy.

"Well, I ain't s-scared no more," said Edison. "Him and his k-kin don't deserve that t-tree."

Truman remembered the night of his going-away party, the night they'd stood up to Boss and his dad, the Grand Dragon of the Klan. But Edison seemed extra-angry.

"Did he do something to you too?" asked Truman.

Edison's eyes grew dark. "He took away the p-pool."

"He what?"

Edison stared down at Boss and couldn't find the words.

"Last summer," said Big Boy. "Me and Edison and Charlie McCants snuck into the community pool at night. It was a real scorcher and no one could sleep. So Charlie had the idea of going swimming at night, since, you know, they don't allow coloreds in there."

"And what's Boss got to do with it?" asked Truman.

"Well, after we did that all week, Boss found out about it and mentioned it to his dad," said Big Boy. "His dad had the city council drain the pool for the summer."

"What on earth for? Did you vandalize it?"

"Naw. It was on account of Edison and Charlie swam in it."

Truman knew how things were in the South, but still, closing the pool just because two black boys touched the water? He just shook his head. "You sure you didn't do anything to the pool? You didn't even *pee* in it?"

Edison snuck a sideways glance at Truman. "I'd never do no such th-thing."

Big Boy stared down the hill at Boss dragging the tree. "You know, certain people on the city council don't like the idea of their kids swimming with certain kids like, well, um, Edison and Charlie."

"You mean colored kids?" asked Truman.

Edison started heading down the hill with a fierce look on his face. He'd take that tree back all by himself if he had to.

"Hold on, Edison. Think about this," said Truman. "People around here don't take kindly to Negroes stepping out of place."

"T-Truman, I've done kept my p-place my whole life and it ain't got me n-nowhere."

"That's not true," said Truman. "You have us! We're all friends here."

Edison thought about it. "Out here, m-maybe. But if'n we all walk into town, we can't act like f-friends."

Edison was right. Monroeville was no place for white boys to be chumming around with black kids.

"Never mind that. Look," said Big Boy, pointing.

Boss had come to a shack on the other side of the gulley and leaned the tree against the back of it. Then he walked around to the front and went inside.

They all looked at one another. "Let's go steal it back," said Truman. "For Edison."

"And T-Truman," said Edison.

"I just want to get this over with," said Big Boy.

When they reached the other side of the gully, they snuck up behind a rock and peeked over the edge like soldiers about to lead a charge. The tree was right there within reach.

"You were right. Sure is a p-pretty tree, Mr. T-Truman," said Edison.

"Between the three of us, we should be able to carry it back to the farm," whispered Big Boy. "That is, if Boss don't come out and kill us."

Truman stared at the tree. It wasn't just a dream. It *was* the perfect tree. Boss had to have known he'd claimed it; why else would he have taken it? "Finders keepers. That's the rule, right? We're just taking back what's ours."

"He can get his own d-dang t-tree," said Edison.

They ran over to it, scrambling across the dirt. When they reached the tree, they could hear Boss and his dad yelling at each other inside the shack.

"Serves him right," said Truman. All he could think about was their encounter with Boss's dad, Catfish, when he was the Grand Dragon of the Klan. "How can they believe in Christmas and be in the Klan at the same time?"

Tru grabbed the base of the trunk. It was much bigger and heavier that he'd thought. Edison lunged to help, but Big Boy beat him to the punch.

"I got it," Big Boy said. "You take up the other end."

Edison grumbled and went to the top of the tree. Big Boy attempted to lift the trunk; he grunted but refused to admit it was too heavy. "Let's go," he hissed.

Truman moved to the middle position. "Everyone lift and let's go before Boss comes out again," he said.

They lifted and struggled a few steps before realizing how awkward carrying a tree really was. No wonder Jennings Sr. always brought one of the mules. "Shoulda brought a dang mule," said Big Boy.

"A mule's just trouble," said Truman.

The bark scraped at Tru's soft hands. Big Boy kept getting scratched and poked by the pine needles. The only one who didn't seem to mind was Edison.

"Faster, faster," Truman kept saying.

"We're going as fast as we can," Big Boy growled.

When they reached the ravine, they decided to let gravity do the work and rolled it carefully down the hill. Unfortunately, they had to carry it up the other side.

"That Boss sure is a strong one," said Big Boy, out of breath. "I'm starting to think some of those other trees are looking pretty good."

"Me t-too," said Edison, even though he didn't want to agree with Big Boy.

"It's this one or nothing," said Truman. "Keep your eyes on the prize."

A half hour later, they were over the top of the hill and finally out of sight of Mudtown. "It's all downhill from here," said Truman.

How right he was. At the bottom of the hill stood Boss.

14
Face-Off

Boss was even bigger, uglier, and meaner than he had been the last time Truman had laid eyes on him. A tangle of thick matted black hair sat on top of his head like the knotty scrub brush that littered the forest behind Jenny's house. He was bigger than any fourteen-year-old should be. If his teeth were any more yellow, they'd be corn kernels.

"We should run," said Truman.

"I reckon you're right, but he's blocking our way home," said Big Boy.

"Or we c-could stand fer what b-be ours," said Edison.

"Or we could run to town," suggested Big Boy.

Edison stared daggers at Boss. "I ain't a-afraid. There's m-more of us than him."

"He don't look too happy, though," said Big Boy.

"I'm t-tired of r-running," said Edison as he headed down the hill.

"Are you tired of breathing too?" shouted Big Boy.

"Let me talk to him," Truman said as he went after Edison.

Big Boy sighed as his two friends went to their certain doom. "Fine," he said, joining Truman. "But don't come crying to me if he kills us."

"If he kills us, you won't hear a peep from me," Truman answered.

They hurried to catch up to Edison.

The look on Boss's face was that of an evil kid in a candy store: So many tasty choices to tear into.

Edison stopped about ten feet short of Boss and brandished his shovel in front of him. Boss snorted. "You might as well dig yourself a grave if you think you're going to steal my tree. Boys like you disappear for less."

"It's *my* tree," said Truman. "I had a claim on it."

Boss didn't recognize Truman, who was dressed in Big Boy's farmer clothes.

"Us too," said Edison and Big Boy together. They glanced at each other and almost smiled.

Boss shook his head. "And since when do coons fight white boys' battles?"

Edison took a step forward and raised the shovel over his head.

"Edison!" Big Boy barged in front of him. "He's baitin' you. Don't fall for it."

Boss spat on the ground. "I don't know what's worse, a coon lover or a—"

"Wait!" said Truman. "That's *my* tree. I claimed it with *my* belt. You can have any other tree, but I want *that* one. I need it."

It took Boss a second to put it together. That voice. He'd never seen Truman without a suit, and the last time he'd seen him was four years ago, when his hair was longer. Then it came to him, along with a mean, squirrely grin.

"Shrimp." Bingo.

"I have no beef with you, Boss." Truman was having a hard time standing his ground.

"But I got one with *you*." Boss pushed Big Boy and Edison aside like they were flies pestering him. He towered over Truman.

Truman flinched and spat out, "It's just a tree. You can have any other one, but this one's *mine*—"

Boss put his big sweaty hand over Truman's face and leaned in. "Because of you and your friends, my daddy lost his job as Grand Dragon. That was the only thing he ever wanted in life. What y'all done turned him into a real bad drunk."

Truman could see through Boss's meaty fingers that he sported a black eye.

"And when he's unhappy, *I'm* unhappy."

Truman felt the hand tightening on his head. He shut his eyes and tried to pull on Boss's arm, but it was like hanging on a branch—he was going nowhere. The hand squeezed tighter and tighter and all he could think about was his head exploding like a water balloon.

"Uncle!" Truman cried out. "Uncle!"

Boss growled, "Your uncle ain't gonna help you now—"

There was a crunch and Truman thought it was his skull being crushed. Instead, Boss's hand slid off his face, followed by a giant thud.

When Truman opened his eyes, he saw Boss lying in the mud with red drops next to his head and Nelle Harper Lee standing behind him with a big branch in her hand.

"Holy cow, Nelle! You killed him!" said Big Boy.

Nelle dropped the branch and blinked like she'd just woken up from a dream. "What happened?"

"You c-clobbered Boss Henderson, that's wh-what happened!" said Edison.

"And you saved my skin," said Truman, rubbing his head. "What're you doing out here?"

Nelle stood over Boss. "I came by the farm to drop off some clothes from Brother, but I just missed you. I followed y'all to see what you were up to. When I saw Boss threatening you," she said quietly, "I had to do something."

"Thanks, Nelle," said Truman.

They all gathered around Boss, who wasn't moving. "Is he breathing?" asked Big Boy.

"I seen a d-dead man once and he looked just like th-that . . ." said Edison.

"We should leave. Before anyone sees us," said Truman, looking around. Luckily, they were obscured by the forest.

"I just meant to stun him so you could get away," said Nelle. "I didn't mean . . ."

Truman stared at his attacker. "It was self-defense, Nelle. We'll all back you on that."

"What do you mean?" she asked.

"If and when the sheriff finds out," said Big Boy.

"The sheriff?"

Edison was wide-eyed with fear. "I be more w-worried 'bout the others, Miss N-Nelle."

"The others?" she asked blankly.

Edison looked over his shoulder. "Boss's p-pa. And the K-Klan."

"But it was self-defense," said Truman again.

Big Boy paced. "We need to see A.C. He'll know what to do," he said, staring at Boss's limp body. "I ain't never seen a dead person before."

"He's right," said Truman. "A.C.'s got a way with fixing problems." He glanced at Nelle, who was lost in thought.

"What about the t-tree?" asked Edison.

They all glared at it lying in the dirt. "Stupid tree," said Truman. He didn't even want it now. Clearly, it was cursed too.

15
Nelle in Trouble

Monroeville was beginning to look like Christmas. A Santa was ringing his bell in front of the drugstore; workers were hanging lights around the square; kids had heard it might even snow for the first time in their lives and were eyeing the sole sled in the hardware-store window. And Nelle Harper was in trouble.

They left Boss where he lay and headed to town. It took them a good while because Nelle fell into a state of numbness just thinking about telling A.C. He had dreams of her going to law school one day, and that'd be a pretty tough thing to do from jail. Truman held her hand all the way to the town center.

After starting and stopping several times to argue about whether they should own up to their predicament or hightail it into the hills, they finally reached A.C.'s office and plodded up the stairs, each step heavier than the last. His office stood ominously at the end of the hallway.

Nelle had her hand on the doorknob when they heard A.C. inside saying to someone, "Is he dead?"

Big Boy looked at Nelle and gulped. "How could they already know?" he whispered.

"Not yet," said another voice. "But he's just hanging on. I don't imagine it'll be much longer."

Nelle started to panic. "They already know!" she whispered. "I'm done for, done for!"

The door suddenly swung open and Sheriff Farrish stood there staring at them, his hand on the pearl-handled revolver in his leather belt.

"What in heaven's name is going on here?" he barked.

Nelle turned pale and swooned.

Truman cowered into a sniveling mess. "It was self-defense!" he shouted. "I just wanted my tree back!"

When Nelle came to her senses a minute later, she was lying on a leather couch in A.C.'s office, where he was wiping her brow with a cool washcloth.

"She's back," said A.C., relieved. "Now maybe you want to tell me what this is all about? We've all had a tough couple of days. But today seems even worse. A man was beaten and will probably die, all for a few dollars and some change, it seems."

Edison spoke up. "We didn't s-steal no money, sir! It was all about the t-tree!"

Now A.C. was really confused. "You robbed the Northrup general store?"

Edison scrunched his face up. "Mr. Lee? We didn't rob no store."

"Well, just what in Sam Hill are you on about?" asked A.C.

Big Boy started hopping up and down. "Oh my God! I can't believe it! Look!" he shouted.

Everyone turned and saw Big Boy pointing out the window. "He's *alive!*" he said excitedly. Truman and Edison ran over and gasped at what they saw.

There, getting out of a flatbed pickup truck, was Boss, upright and very much not dead. He had a bloody rag tied around his head. His pa, Catfish Henderson, helped him as they walked up to Doc Carter's place.

"Sweet L-Lord, it's a m-miracle," said Edison when he saw for himself. "Nelle's not a k-killer!"

Her father had had enough. "Explain yourselves."

Truman spoke up. "It's all my doing, sir. I put us in a situation with Boss and he ended up trying to tear my head off. Things got out of hand, but Nelle stood up for me."

There was a knock on the door and everyone jumped. A.C. went to the door, and someone handed him a note.

A strange expression came over Truman's face. "Oh no."

"What's wrong?" whispered Nelle.

Tru shook his head. "You may not be a killer. But you're go-ing to die anyways."

Big Boy caught on. "*Ooh*, you mean . . . now that Boss is alive, he's going to kill her for killing him?"

"Maybe he g-got amnesia from getting hit on his head! Maybe h-he'll never remember you d-did it!" Edison said.

Nelle looked at him. "Well, knucklehead, he didn't see *me*. The last ones he saw were you three."

Truman, Big Boy, and Edison all gulped at once. "She's right. He's gonna come for us," said Big Boy.

"We'll have to leave town," said Truman. "We'll run away and join the circus."

"You all ain't going nowhere," said Nelle. "You can't keep running from everything, Tru."

"Children," said A.C.

"You want us to die?" said Truman. "Because Boss is gonna kill all of us. Then he'll come looking for you when one of us squeals under duress."

"*What?*" said Nelle.

"Children," said A.C. again.

Edison was in a daze from all the excitement. "Maybe it were better when B-Boss was d-dead. Least then we coulda got that Christmas t-tree—"

"Children!"

They all stopped and turned to A.C., who was holding up a letter. "I don't know what kind of shenanigans you all have been up to this morning, but I have a real death on my hands.

112

Mr. Northrup has passed. And the sheriff wants me to go over to Lower Peach. So I suggest you just go home and let sleeping dogs lie."

"But—" said Nelle.

"But nothing, Nelle Harper. I'll give these boys a ride back to the farm, then we'll be on our way."

"We?" asked Nelle.

He put his hand on her shoulder. "You're coming with me."

16
The Call

Nelle was quietly fretting the whole way back to the farm. When they passed the forest, Truman wondered about the tree. It had to be just lying there.

"Don't even think about it," said Big Boy. "I've had enough for one day."

As they neared the farmhouse, they saw Jenny and Mary Ida sternly waiting on the front porch.

"Uh-oh, we must be in trouble," said Big Boy.

"They don't know anything," said Truman. "And I plan to keep it that way."

He paused and looked at A.C. "Sorry, Mr. Lee. I just think the less said, the better. For Nelle's sake."

A.C. came to a stop in front of the house and turned to Truman. "Little white lies are a slippery slope, Truman. If you're not careful, they turn into bigger ones, and the next thing you know, you've created a landslide. You boys keep out of trouble, hear?"

"Yes, sir," all three said in unison.

They tumbled out of the car and Truman paused before closing the door. He smiled at Nelle. "See you soon?"

She nodded but seemed worried.

Jenny came down from the porch looking like a rooster ready to fight. "Truman, what have you done?"

So many possible answers flew through his head that, for once, he was speechless.

"Miss Jenny," A.C. called from the car. "I just want you to know again how sorry I am for your troubles of late. I'm making it my mission to help you rebuild. I have a client who's a contractor and will give you more than fair price. And I also have several clients who do carpentry work."

Jenny had more on her mind than her house. "Thank you, Mr. Lee. But as I said, I can do just fine by myself."

"I know you can," said A.C. "Perhaps I'm more worried about my honor. If I go to my grave knowing what I did . . ." He couldn't finish.

Jenny could see the pain in his face. She reached into the car and extended her hand to him. "Mr. Lee, you have done more for this community than most. There is no sense in beating yourself up over this. You want to do penance? Fine. Continue to do what you're doing: helping those who cannot help themselves. That is what you do best. The rest of us will be fine."

He nodded. He knew when a negotiation was over. "I understand," he said as he started up the car. "Be kind to the boy," he added. "He's had a hard day."

And with that, he drove off the farm.

Jenny stood there watching the car go. Then she turned to Truman with her hands on her hips. "Well? Don't you have something to tell me?"

Truman shrugged, not wanting to get into the whole tree story.

"I received a telegram from your mother," said Jenny.

"Oh." That. It would all come out now.

"I got to g-go," said Edison quickly. He turned and skedaddled out to the fields as fast as he could.

Mary Ida glared at Big Boy. "Uh, I gotta tend to the fields before the sun disappears," said Big Boy, leaving Truman all alone.

Truman sighed. He knew he had to confess.

Mary Ida went inside. Jenny had an odd mix of disappointment and concern on her face.

"How did she find me?" asked Truman.

Jenny frowned. "Is that all you have to say? The school tracked your mother down in Cuba. She knew this was the only place you would go. The school said there would be stern consequences for your actions."

The Call

Jenny didn't have a motherly bone in her body. She was much more the father in charge, the one who put food on the table and created order in her family. But Truman couldn't help it. He grabbed her around the waist and held on tight. He could feel the air go out of her, for she did not like to be touched.

"You don't know what it was like up there in that military school," Truman said. "The sergeants yelled at me day and night, called me mama's boy, sissy, said I ran like a girl. They made fun of my Southern accent, and then when I changed it, they made fun of that too. When I told them I'm a writer, it was always 'So you think you're better than us?'"

Jenny's hands came to rest on his shoulders. She didn't know what to say.

Truman sniffled. "The boys there were even worse. When the lights went out and the night watch moved on . . . the things they did to me."

Truman shuddered at the memories. "The last straw was during the fight drill—they made me the practice dummy. Told me to take it like a man."

He lifted his shirt to show his bruises.

Jenny sighed and stroked his fine hair. "Honestly, I don't know why your mother would do such a thing. Sending you of all people to that horrid place."

She bent down and put her hand on his face. "I telegrammed her to say you'd be staying here through New Year's and then you'd go back home. I think she needs time to cool off, don't you?"

Ten days. He'd bought himself a ten-day reprieve. "They're not going to make me go back to that place, are they? I can't. I will run away forever, I swear it."

Jenny nodded. "I'll do what I can, but she is your legal guardian. Besides, I had to throw away that dirty old uniform. Little Bit said it was too damaged to mend." She winked, then wiped her hands on her apron. "I'll try to talk some sense into your mother. She was always a foolhardy child. I think you irk her because you are as stubborn as she is."

He wiped his nose. "Was she worried, at least?"

Jenny brushed his blond hair off his forehead. "You go inside and wash up." She felt his forehead again. "You're warm. Probably getting a fever after standing out in this weather all night and day. You best plan on staying in for a while. In the meantime, you focus on Christmas. It's the one thing that will take our minds off our troubles."

He nodded. He was tired of the curse. Maybe if he stayed put, nothing else bad would happen.

Big Boy walked Edison back to his shack. "Don't worry. If you stay here on the farm, Boss won't dare get us," said Big Boy.

"B-but fer how long?" asked Edison.

Big Boy scratched his head. "Until we're old enough to leave Alabama?"

Edison didn't like that answer. "Fer all he know, *you* c-conked him on the head."

"How could I? I was right in front of him," said Big Boy. "I sure hope he don't remember a thing . . ."

Edison paced back and forth in front of his chicken coop. "How we gonna f-find out what h-he knows? If he has a-amnesia, then we're f-free. If he think a tree b-branch broke off and c-conked him, we're also f-free."

"I ain't gonna ask. *You* gonna talk to him?" said Big Boy.

Big Boy started pacing too. "We need s-someone he won't never beat up. S-somebody he so scared of . . ." mumbled Edison. "I c-can't think of no one."

Big Boy snapped his fingers. "What if instead we got someone so nice and so old, he wouldn't dare kill them?"

Sook tiptoed into Big Boy's room, where Truman was lying in bed. She was carrying a tray covered with his granny-square blanket.

Truman pretended to be asleep.

"I brought you something. Your favorite." She sat on the edge of the bed and put the tray down. When she pulled off the cloth, Truman opened his eyes and saw a glass of warm milk and three cookies that looked like furry white mounds, each topped with a red cherry.

"Ambrosia macaroons!" he said excitedly. "I dreamed of these when I was away, Sook."

Sook patted his hand. She had dark circles under her eyes, and her nose was red, but she seemed determined to be chipper.

"Now, Trueheart, drink up. This'll warm you and put some spirit back in your belly. And those cookies I made special just for you. Believe me, in this kitchen, that ain't no small feat. And here," she said, holding up the granny square. "An old friend."

Truman took it and pressed it to his cheek. It was clean and fresh again. "You're the best, Sook. But you know I'm too old for this now, right?"

She shrugged. "Shucks, you're never too old for a granny square. But I'll hold on to it for you if'n you don't want it." She reached for it, but Truman pulled it away.

"I can keep it . . . for now," he said slyly.

He took a sip of the warm milk and let it trickle down his throat. He hadn't realized just how cold he'd been since coming back to Monroeville. Snuggled in a warm quilt, he could feel the ice melt off his bones.

"I'm glad you ran away," said Sook.

Truman looked at her. "Jenny told you? And the others?"

She winked. "We all ran away at some point, Tru. The good thing is, you ran *here*."

He nodded and took a big bite of a cookie.

Sook elbowed him gently in the side. "We have so much to do, Tru. We only have three days till Christmas, and it's going to be twice as busy this year. We have presents to make, decorations to hang, and most special of all—"

"Fruitcakes," Truman said, grinning.

"You read my mind, Tru. Let the others worry about everything else. We know what we have to do. It'll be just like before, you'll see."

Truman hugged her. "Ever since I left, that's all I ever wanted."

"Well, even if you lose everything, they can't take Christmas away from you. You rest up. Tomorrow, we have someplace to go."

Truman knew that meant a trip to the Indian reservation for the special magic ingredient in her fruitcake recipe.

17

Incident at Murder Creek

Nelle didn't know why A.C. was taking her to a crime scene. Especially at twilight. But she liked being with him, whether it was helping with his duties at the *Monroe Journal* or down at the Baptist church or just watching him from the balcony at the courthouse. His mind was always elsewhere, just as it was now. At least in the car, he couldn't totally ignore her. Even if he wasn't speaking.

"Word," she said. It was a game they sometimes played, where you gave two clues for the other to guess a word: the first letter and the number of letters in the word. "*T.* And four," she added.

It was easier than mentioning the altercation with Boss.

He mulled it over and arched an eyebrow toward her. *"Talk,"* he answered. Easier said than done.

"Your mother . . ." he began. He mumbled to himself as if there were a conversation going on in his head. Nelle waited a good twenty seconds before he added, "She was pretty rattled by the fire. As was I. I still can't believe . . ."

"It wasn't your fault, Daddy," said Nelle.

He paused. She rarely called him that. "Still, I shouldn't have . . ." He put his hand on her knee. "I know you were rattled too. I'm sorry I wasn't there for you. But you're like your sisters — self-sufficient and strong-willed. I have to focus on your mother now."

"The treehouse burned down, did you know that, A.C.?" she said.

He made an odd face, like his train of thought had just derailed. "No, honey. I suppose I didn't notice. Things were . . . out of hand that night. Your mother had a pretty bad episode."

"I was there," she said.

"Yes, but she has it in her mind that the fire . . . might have been her fault, that she was thinking bad thoughts. Sometimes the things she says . . ." He waited a minute for Nelle to pipe up but she stayed silent.

Finally, she said, "Maybe the fire was caused by the electrical? Jenny was always saying they had wiring problems ever since they installed lights."

He shrugged. "I didn't hear that. When I was standing

outside trying to keep the flames from coming over the wall, I noticed the winds were carrying embers from our fireplace toward their roof. I could kick myself for not fixing the grate in the chimney last summer."

She didn't want to say it, but when she'd climbed up to the treehouse for the last time, she'd noticed the same thing. Wanting to change the subject, she thought first about the holidays. "We haven't talked about presents or anything. For Christmas, I mean."

A.C. nodded. "Sometimes I forget you're still a little girl. Have you made a list for Santa?"

"I ain't little and you know I don't believe in Santa. Money is tight. And I don't need presents."

A.C. cleared his throat. "It's just that I have other things to deal with right now. Christmas seems a million miles away. Ah, here we are."

The car headed toward an old bridge that led to the other side of the waterway, where the general store stood. A sign was nailed to the rail of the bridge announcing the small river's name: Murder Creek.

Nelle hadn't been out that way in a long time but still thought it strange that someone would call a creek that.

A.C. parked the car, keeping the headlamps aimed at the bridge and storefront. When he got out, Nelle grabbed a flashlight from the glove compartment. As they crossed the old rickety bridge, she could see the general store on the other embankment.

It was what you call a riverfront store, where folks could pull up in their boats, load supplies, and float on downriver to the next stop. The store was decorated with hand-painted signs of Santa drinking Coca-Cola.

The creek was not terribly wide but it was deep, and Nelle remembered going there once with A.C. when she was younger. He had helped out the store's owner, Mr. Northrup, a former riverboat gambler who'd found religion and become an honest man. She remembered he was nice, gave her a lollipop. He'd preferred to pay A.C. with groceries and whatnot. A.C. took only enough for supper and said they were square. When she asked why he didn't take more, he said an honest man only takes what the favor was worth.

An older colored man in overalls and glasses was trying to sweep the frost off the wooden bridge. When he saw A.C. and Nelle walking toward him, he stood to the side and removed his hat, even though there was a brisk wind coming off the water. As they passed, he said, "Sir, miss," and stood that way until they were clear across.

"I don't like when they do that," said Nelle. "I ain't royalty."

"That's what colored folks do down here, Nelle. It's been a custom ever since I was a boy."

The sheriff was smoking a cigarette on the porch as a deputy was talking to a distraught woman. A.C. stopped short of the store.

"You best wait here," he said to Nelle.

"Why? I'm a good detective. Maybe I can help," she said.

He placed his hand on her head. "This isn't a game, Nelle." He turned and walked over to the sheriff.

Nelle watched A.C. and the sheriff walk through the crime. From a distance, it seemed like the sheriff was reenacting the whole event from start to finish. She could see him pretending to be Mr. Northrup, sitting on the porch, having a smoke, when some river men came up from the banks. Then he acted like someone was trying to rob him, sticking his hands in the air. There was a struggle, as evidenced by the stool and boxes overturned on their sides, and then he was whacked—*boom*—and fell.

When Nelle saw that, a chill crawled up her spine. The sheriff was now on his knees, dragging himself toward the door while his imaginary robbers fled back to the river.

He pointed her way and she quickly looked down to avoid his eyes. She focused on the ground—in particular, on a dark spot in the lightness of the frost. She aimed the light at it.

Blood.

She gulped and stepped aside to see a trail of footprints heading back to the river. Between the frost and the mud, she could see it was more than one person. Her eyes went to the dock and she found herself walking toward it. When the footsteps sloped down toward the water, she spotted scuff marks, like someone had fallen and slid a few feet down the embankment and onto the dock.

She carefully walked down and studied where that person had gotten back up. She could see that one footprint was messed up, like the person was dragging his foot.

Something caught her eye. She glanced back at the store, where A.C. was still asking questions and the sheriff was going through the motions again. She bent down, wiped some mud away with her hand, and picked up a little plastic figurine: Santa, riding in his sleigh.

She dipped it in the icy water to get the mud off and happened to glance up and see the old man on the bridge staring at her.

When their eyes met, he turned away and started sweeping again.

"Nelle!"

She turned around to see her dad waving her back. "Let's go."

She stuffed the figurine into her coat pocket and scrambled up the embankment, her hands frozen from frigid water and air. When she reached him, he was writing in his little notebook.

She watched the sheriff as he righted the stool and boxes on the porch.

"Is Mr. Northrup in there?" she asked.

A.C. stopped writing. "No, he was taken to the hospital. He . . . passed away there." He paused with his pencil poised over his notepad, then began to write again.

"I . . ." she started. "I hit Boss Henderson on the head today."

A.C. looked up at her.

"When we came to your office, we thought I had, you know . . . killed him," she muttered.

"What?" he said sternly.

"We didn't, of course. We saw him alive from your window. Just banged up," she added.

"Why would you do such a thing?" he asked.

"He was hurting Truman. I had to step in," she said honestly.

A.C. sighed. "Sometimes I think I don't pay enough attention to you. Maybe all the dealings with your mother somehow make you angry—"

"I ain't angry!" she said, then realized she'd yelled. "Sorry."

"Sorry is what you will be," he said, "if you don't go over to Boss's tomorrow and apologize."

Nelle's jaw dropped.

"I mean it," he said. "Do you doubt my word?"

She'd felt the sting of his belt before. "No, sir."

"Good." He returned to his notebook, struggling to write in the dark. Nelle shined her light on it.

"Did he say anything?" she asked.

He paused. "Who? Mr. Northrup? No. His mind was too blurry to remember the perpetrator."

"*Sss,*" she said.

"What?"

"Perpetrator*s,*" she said. "There was two of 'em."

She pointed the light at the tracks on the ground, which she had walked all over. She realized her mistake. "I saw two pairs of boot prints leading down to the creek."

He tapped his pencil against the notepad. "How do you know it wasn't one man coming and then going back again? Or maybe the sheriff walked down and back."

She looked at the sheriff, who was leaning on a stool finishing his cigarette. "Maybe you should ask the man on the bridge. I think he knows something."

A.C. glanced at the man, who was watching them. The man immediately turned and began to sweep again.

A.C. closed his notebook and returned it to his coat pocket. Nelle followed as he walked back to the bridge.

The man was sweeping his way across the already swept bridge. When the footsteps grew close, he once again stepped aside and removed his cap. "Sir, miss. Merry Christmas to you both."

"And to you," said A.C., studying the man's face. "Say, do I know you?"

Nelle pointed her light at him and the man held his hat tighter to his chest and swallowed. She could see his breath in the cold night air. "I knows who you are, sir. You have no reason to knows me."

"And yet, you are familiar . . . Are you of relations to Miss Little Bit?"

The man frowned. "No, sir."

"Mm. Perhaps Edison's father . . . Cousin?"

He shook his head. "I have seen you in court, sir. From the balcony."

He nodded. "Ah, that's probably it. Any particular case?" he asked.

The man paused, shifting his feet. "Not that I can recalls, sir. 'Cept the one about the young boy, Mr. Truman, and his folks."

He stood there uncomfortably, his feet on the edge of the bridge. There was no wall stopping him from falling ten feet into the freezing water.

"You seen the two fellas that done this?" asked Nelle.

The man's eyes went wide. A.C. shot Nelle a look. She backed down.

"I . . . I didn't see no one. I-I wasn't h-here when they got in the b-boat," he stuttered.

Nelle looked at her father. A.C. sighed and took his notebook back out.

18
Voodoo

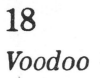

That night, Truman awoke to the sensation of someone breathing on him. He heard snipping and felt a little tug on his hair. When he opened his eyes, Little Bit was in his face holding a pair of scissors in one hand and a clump of blond hair in the other.

His blond hair.

He sat up and grabbed his head to see if he was bald. "What're you doing, Little Bit?" he said excitedly. Big Boy grumbled in his sleep and rolled over.

"*Shh*, Mr. Truman. You don't want to wake the spirits." Next to a candle on the nightstand, she had three glass bottles—one red, one blue, and one green. Inside were crosses made of red root and peppermint. She took several strands of his hair and dropped them into each bottle.

"Why are you doing that?" he whispered.

"Gonna help you break that curse of yours," she said, matter-of-fact.

Truman was surprised. "How do you know about that?" he asked.

"Little Bit knows everything, honey. It don't take no fortuneteller to see bad is sticking to you like a fly to flypaper." She reached down and pulled up a cotton sack and placed it on the bed.

"I'd do anything to change things—" He froze when he spotted the bag moving. Truman instinctively knew there was a snake inside the sack. "Little Bit, are you *crazy?* You can't bring a snake in here!"

Little Bit wasn't troubled. "Hush. Don't you worry none. I slipped it some of Dr. Yah-Yah's magic snake potion, so it's sleepy."

She opened the bag and looked inside. Satisfied, she reached in—

"No!" said Truman.

She pulled out a cottonmouth by the neck. Truman felt faint and closed his eyes. Big Boy snored.

"Relax, child. We're just borrowing some of its venom for the spell. When it wakes up again, it'll be home in the swamps like nothing ever happened."

Truman opened his eyes. Little Bit held the snake's mouth

open and pressed its fangs against the lip of each bottle until small drops of venom had fallen onto every cross.

"I never saw a cottonmouth close up before," he said, touching its skin. "Except for the one that bit me on the knee when I was little."

"I remember," she said. He had been an hour away from home and would have died had it not been for a traveling gypsy who came upon him. The man took a live chicken from his wagon and cut it, then held the chicken's wound against Truman's bite until the blood and heat drew out all the poison. The chicken turned green and Truman lived.

When she was done, Little Bit gently returned the snake to the sack. "Good night, my sister." She then took out three red ribbons and tied them around the lips of the bottles.

"Do you think it will help?" Truman asked.

Little Bit reached over and yanked open the window next to the bed. The freezing night air rushed in, and on the outside stood Bama.

Truman jumped. "What are you doing out there!"

Little Bit handed the bottles to Bama. "I know a thing or two about curses too," Bama said, her breath visible. She reached for the willow-tree branches that hung down near the window.

"Now take the end of the branch and dip it into the bottle and tie it off."

"I know, I know," said Bama. "This ain't my first rodeo." She grabbed the end of a branch, stuffed it into a bottle, and tied the bottle to the branch until it hung down like an ornament. She did the same for each bottle. "This here a blooming tree," she said to Truman. "The bottles draw the evil spirits and trap 'em. Then you be free of the curse."

"Course, you'll have to sleep with the windows open so the spirits can leave your body at night," said Little Bit.

Truman watched the bottles gently clink against each other in the breeze. "I must be dreaming," he said.

Little Bit blew some white powder into his face, making him cough. "Hey—"

As Truman wiped the powder from his eyes, Little Bit began chanting some mysterious words he had never heard before.

"Is that it?" he asked, annoyed.

Little Bit patted him on the head. "Soon, your problems will be done and gone. You'll see."

When she shut the door on her way out, Big Boy finally stirred. "*Wha*—? Why are you up?" he asked sleepily.

"Just waiting for things to change," he said. "Go back to sleep." Truman sat in the dark and waited to feel different. But deep down inside, he still felt the same.

19
Restless

Nelle couldn't sleep. Her mind was racing. Seeing Truman brought back so many memories. Then the incident with Boss, followed by the visit to a crime scene — she couldn't stop thinking.

She sat up and looked out her window at what used to be Truman's house. Under the crisp moonlight, it was a hulking black mess. When he had lived there, they'd set up the can-to-can call line from her room to the fort to his room so they could talk after dark. They shared thoughts about cases they were working on, story ideas inspired by dreams, and, most of all, secrets. She had secrets she hadn't shared, though, and knew he had some too. The thing he said about his first kiss threw her for a loop. She supposed she somehow felt jealous that it hadn't been her — until he said it had been with another boy. Then she didn't know what to think.

Nelle had not kissed anyone until Truman had kissed her. A.C. once tried to have a talk with her about boys, but it was so awkward, it hurt.

Still, she wished she could talk to Truman now. She missed his friendship, missed that line that connected them late at night when everyone was asleep, when it seemed they were the only two alive.

She kept thinking about the incident at the creek with the old man and how she got A.C. to find out that the man had seen two others. "They was colored men" was all he could see due to them being bundled up against the cold. One seemed older, needed help getting onto their boat, a little handmade raft of some sort.

"Why didn't you tell the sheriff?" A.C. asked. The man frowned and said that him just saying it was two black men would turn everyone he knew into a suspect. Including himself.

She saw the look in the man's eyes and knew he felt helpless. She'd felt that way more than once in her life and was sorry she'd gotten him to reveal his secret.

Nelle heard the piano tinkling in the living room. It was her mother, sleepless as she was most nights. A.C. usually let her play awhile even though he knew it bothered the neighbors.

Nelle padded down the hallway to the living room until she saw her mother playing by candlelight in her nightgown. A blanket had slid off her shoulders onto the floor. Nelle tiptoed in, not wanting to startle her. She was playing a song called "All of Me," which meant she was in a good mood.

When Nelle put the blanket back on her shoulders, her mother stopped playing and looked at her. She almost never did that anymore — really looked anyone in the eyes like she used to when Nelle was little, before the troubles began.

"Hi, Mama," she said.

Her mother smiled, felt her cheek with her hand. "Hello, Nelle . . ."

Hearing her name come from her mother surprised her. She hadn't called her Nelle for a long time. Her mother mostly ignored her or was upset at something that had nothing to do with Nelle. But now she was back.

"Ain't you freezing out here? Don'tcha want to go back to bed?" asked Nelle.

"Oh, no, honey. I'm fine." She began to play again, this time a Christmas song. "Have you written your letter to Santa yet?"

Nelle didn't know what to say. She'd stopped believing when she was six, and that was when A.C. started a tradition where everyone would make one present and they'd stack them all under a tree and each would pick one, blindfolded. Which meant sometimes Nelle received things intended for A.C. or Brother, like a hand-sewn tie or men's cologne.

"Not yet," she answered, humoring her.

"Well, don't wait too long. Santa is very busy . . ."

She played a few more bars of music but stopped suddenly and slumped her shoulders. "Why don't you go play with Truman and let me be?"

Nelle stared at the darkened husk of Truman's house through the window. She wished she could.

20
The Favor

After spending the early morning tending to the crops, Edison and Big Boy stood on the back porch of the farmhouse looking into the kitchen. Little Bit and Bama were standing side by side prepping food on a table. In a way, voodoo had brought them a little closer together. They were both chopping and slicing, rolling and slapping. When Little Bit cooked, she liked to sing and tap her feet. Bama playfully elbowed her whenever she moved too close; Little Bit's hip pushed back the other way.

Meanwhile, Sook busied herself looking for certain ingredients, pulling out pots and pans, and making a list.

"*Psst,*" said Big Boy.

Sook waved her hand as if she were chasing away flies.

"Sook," he whispered.

She stopped writing and cocked her head in his direction. "What you want, Big Boy? Supper's not for a while."

"Can we talk?" he asked.

Little Bit stopped rolling and glanced over her shoulder.

"Busy," said Sook. "Got to start fruitcake production."

Big Boy turned to Edison. "Fruitcakes. That's good."

"I don't c-cares so much fer them myself," said Edison.

Bama's ears pricked up. "Just keep in mind this ain't no bakery, Miss Sook. This here kitchen is fer making supper an' the like."

Little Bit rolled her eyes. "Oh, hush, woman. It's three days to Christmas. Fruitcakes is a family tradition. Let Miss Sook make her cakes."

"Does that mean you'll be going out to see Indian Joe?" asked Big Boy. "Because if you are, we could go too and help. Or maybe even go for you, since I know you don't like to go out, especially when the weather is this nippy."

Sook studied the two. "I wasn't born yesterday, you know. Out with it."

They walked in, looking nervously at Bama and Little Bit.

"Oh, ignore them," said Sook. "They just being catty. They know who butters their bread."

"I butter my own bread," mumbled Little Bit.

"Maybe you be buttering mine before long," cracked Bama.

Edison and Big Boy took Sook by the elbow and led her into the hallway. "Oh boy, this should be good," said Sook.

When they were out of range of the kitchen and of Jenny and Mary Ida in the front room, Big Boy laid everything on the line.

"We need you to, um, talk to someone for us," he said.

"Is it a girl?" she said. "Shucks, honey, you just need to give 'em flowers and a smile."

"No, it's not a girl, Sook. We're in trouble—"

Edison cut him off. "We need s-someone who can t-talk reason into s-somebody else . . ."

"Somebody dangerous," added Big Boy.

"And b-big."

Sook looked at the two and shook her head. "Now, why would I do that? I'm just a sweet little old lady."

Big Boy nodded. "Well, that's exactly why. You know Mrs. Henderson?"

Sook furrowed her brow. "Catfish's wife?"

The boys nodded in unison.

She shrugged. "You got problems with Catfish, I can't help ya."

"Not Catfish . . ." Big Boy glanced at Edison.

"His b-boy, Boss," said Edison.

Sook smiled. "Oh, you mean little Catfish? What's his name . . . Peter?"

"We only know him as Boss," said Big Boy. "Because he's like . . . the boss."

"Of everyone. A-and he ain't so l-little," said Edison.

Sook smiled. "He was when I last saw him. Cute little fella. Played piano too. They used ta live over by the cemetery," she recalled.

Big Boy shrugged. "Well, now they're in Mudtown, an' the thing is, he aims to kill me—"

"And m-me—" said Edison.

"And Truman and Nelle while he's at it. And we was wondering—"

"Since y-you knew his m-mama—"

"Maybe you could talk to her and maybe she could talk some sense into him, so maybe he wouldn't, you know, kill us," said Big Boy.

Sook stared at them, wide-eyed. "Now, why on earth would Peter want to kill *you* all?"

"W-well . . ." said Edison. "On account of the Christmas t-tree."

"It's complicated," said Big Boy.

"And maybe because N-Nelle clocked him c-cold with a b-branch—"

"'Cause she was trying to save Truman from getting his head squashed!"

"Which she d-done. But now, since he d-didn't die, he aiming to k-kill us for sure, and we all like to l-live long enough—"

"To see Christmas, at least."

Their eyes pleaded with her like little orphan children's.

Sook took it all in. "Oh my, that is something. Is that why

Tru was in such a state last night? Well, I'd be happy to go talk to Mrs. Henderson if you think it'll help."

The boys exhaled, relieved.

"*If'n* you all go to Indian Joe's and get me what I need for my fruitcakes," said Sook.

Each of them made a face. "But what if Boss sees us?" asked Big Boy.

"Oh, I can go straightaway. I just need a ride," said Sook. "You two can take the mules if you like. You know how those roads are out to the reservation."

Big Boy knew. He'd been near there only once before. Indian Joe was quite a character—a bootlegger and snake farmer. The only people who went out there were folks looking for trouble, whiskey, snakes, or all three.

"Okay," said Big Boy, holding out his hand.

Sook shook it. "Deal."

21
Stubborn Like a Mule

Truman was still sitting in bed, wondering if the curse was gone, when Sook walked in carrying a tray. "Rise and shine, Trueheart. How you feel this morning?" she asked, setting the tray on the nightstand.

"Better, I think. Big Boy told me to sleep in. Said I was kicking and twitching all night," Tru said.

Sook licked her thumb and rubbed it on his cheek. "Why do you have white powder on your face?"

"Oh, that. Little Bit's remedy to make things better." He spotted the tray on which sat two cups of coffee. "Is that for me?"

Sook nodded and sat on his bed. "Don't tell Jenny. She thinks it'll stunt your growth."

Truman shrugged. "Well, she just might be right about that." He took a sip and felt it wash through his system. She'd made it full of milk and sugar, and after he drained the cup, he was wide awake.

"You ever drive a car, Tru?" asked Sook.

Truman laughed. "You mean a real car? I drove bumper cars all the time at this place called Coney Island in New York. It was a real amusement park. Also, Bud used to let me drive his tractor around."

"Good enough for me," she said. "Let's go for a ride."

He gazed out the window. The road was a mess.

"Jenny's going to drive us in this weather?" asked Truman.

"Oh dear, no. She's still asleep. So's Bud. But I promised I'd pay a visit this morning and I'm not walking, so I guess that means you're driving."

Truman looked worried. "I don't think Jenny will like that."

"Oh, hush, we'll be back before she wakes. Just going down the road a bit."

Truman was puzzled. "To see who?"

Sook smiled and winked. "You'll see. Just making a little holiday visit."

"L-look, I can make its ears go d-down," said Edison.

Big Boy had heard the braying of the mule from outside the barn and was in no mood for Edison's antics. It had rained, and the temperature had dropped to freezing overnight. His face

ached from the cold. When Big Boy walked in, Edison was poking the mule in the side with a broom, making her mighty mad.

"I told you, don't be poking Mary. She'll take a bite out of
you for sure," said Big Boy.

"That's Ida. M-Mary don't come near me," Edison answered.
"They b-both been acting up."

Big Boy's dad had named one mule Mary and the other Ida,
after his stubborn but faithful wife. "They're mules, they're supposed to act up," said Big Boy. "Fetch a couple of sacks to sit on.
I ain't riding bareback."

Edison made a face at the mule, making her whinny. "You
know, if we t-took some rope, we could p-prob'ly drag that t-tree
back here."

Big Boy stared at him like he'd lost his marbles. "Are you
crazy? I bet Boss and his daddy's people are waiting to ambush
us. I ain't going back there."

"Just s-sayin'. The t-tree's prob'ly s-still there."

Big Boy shook his head. "Look, Sook is gonna settle this
once and for all so we don't die. You go messing with that tree
again and you might as well turn that hole of yours into a grave."

"It ain't no g-grave. It's my secret p-project," Edison said.
He poked the mule again and she let out a honk in Big Boy's
direction. "That's what I s-say to you."

"You poke that mule again and Boss won't be the only one to
kill you; Mary will."

"Th-that's Ida," mumbled Edison.

"Let's get going before my butt freezes off. It'll take us an hour to get to Indian Joe's now that the road is muddy and frozen over," said Big Boy. He didn't really want to go, but a deal was a deal.

22
Driving Lesson

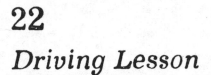

Nelle hated that Big Boy's house didn't have a phone. If she ever wanted to see him and school wasn't in session, she had to ride her bike or get A.C. to give her a lift out to Drewry Road.

But A.C. was busy today and the bike was no good on the sloppy winter roads with their ankle-deep tire ruts, so she had to hoof it to Big Boy's. But if she was going to apologize to Boss today, she needed backup. Wrapped in Bear's old coat, Nelle was steadily getting hotter and hotter as she walked. When she heard a car coming her way and saw Truman's tiny head barely peeking over its steering wheel, Nelle thought she was hallucinating.

She could see Sook holding on for dear life. The car was swerving all over the road. Nelle started to edge over to the side.

She waved at Truman, but since she couldn't see his eyes, he couldn't see her either. Had Sook not yelled "Stop!" Truman might have run her over.

Nelle ended up diving into a bramble of barren huckleberry bushes. Truman skidded to a stop and popped his head over the steering wheel. "Nelle! What are you doing there?"

"What in tarnation!" said Nelle. She wrestled her way out of the bramble. "You coulda kilt me!" she shouted, pulling twigs from her collar. "Who said you could drive that thing?"

"Um, Sook did."

Sook smiled. "Morning, Nelle. You coming to see us?"

Nelle nodded. "Morning, Miss Sook. As a matter of fact, yes." She climbed into the back seat of the car. "Truman, you won't believe what happened. There's been a murder!"

Truman and Sook twisted around, eyes wide. "Who?" they both said.

Nelle grew serious. "Mr. Northrup, at the riverfront store."

Sook crossed herself. "Good Lord. A Christmas murder? That's downright terrible."

But Truman was excited. "Do they know who did it?"

Nelle shook her head. "No. But there was two of 'em. Robbed him of a couple dollars and a loaf of bread. And this." She reached into her pocket and produced the plastic Santa figurine. "I found it at the crime scene."

"That's just terrible," said Sook. "Who would do such a thing during the holidays?"

"I don't think they meant to," said Nelle. "A.C. said a fight

149

broke out and things got out of hand. Maybe they just wanted some food and Mr. Northrup tried to scare 'em off."

Truman looked at Nelle. She had that gleam in her eye, but it was tempered by the fact that this wasn't just a common robbery. A man had lost his life.

"Before you even go thinking about writing a story about this," Nelle said, "A.C. says this ain't a case for children. The sheriff is on it and said we should butt out like everybody else."

"The sheriff," scoffed Truman. "We all know he's lacking in detective skills."

"Truman," said Sook, "don't dilly-dally—we need to get going if we want to be back before everyone wakes up. Nelle, you're welcome to come with us."

"Where you going?"

"Mudtown. To pay a visit. And to extend the Christmas spirit."

"Well, it just so happens that's where I need to go too," said Nelle.

Edison and Big Boy were riding Mary and Ida through the rough woods toward the fish camp on Little River. They had a simple mission: get the secret ingredient for Sook's fruitcake recipe.

Edison and Big Boy had never been down there but they'd certainly heard the stories—Indian Joe was a snake wrangler, a moonshiner, and the type of shady character everyone should avoid. But Sook laughed at such stories, saying it was just rubbish people said about the Indians. The people at the camp were a noble tribe, skilled at the art of fishing, but they needed money to get through the winter. Sook had given Big Boy five dollars and said Joe would know what it was for.

Big Boy was freezing, his teeth chattering. Edison kept flapping his arms and smacking his legs to keep warm. In between, he'd imitate Ida, honking and squealing, just to pass the time.

"Keep doing that and she'll kick you off into the mud," said Big Boy.

"Well, wh-what else is there to do? I g-got to keep my mind off how c-cold it is!" he said.

The so-called path was miserable and slow going. They wound their way up the hill. "Wh-why we going this w-way again instead of taking the m-main road?" asked Edison.

"Because even Boss wouldn't be stupid enough to wander out here," Big Boy answered.

Eventually the sun poked its way through the gray haze of the sky, and the boys made it to the ridge overlooking the fish camp. All was quiet down below; nothing moved except the smoke rising from the chimney of one of the cabins.

"I heard he lets all his s-snakes run free in that cabin so no one will go in and steal his wh-whiskey," said Edison.

"Sook says Joe spreads those rumors himself so he don't have to do it in real life."

"I heard he scalped one of the l-logger men when they tried to c-cut down some of his t-trees," said Edison.

"You been watching too many Westerns. They don't scalp people no more. Sook says—"

"How d-do Sook know? She ever been down h-here?" asked Edison.

Big Boy nodded. "She said she's been going to the fish camp ever since she was a kid."

Edison's eyes grew wide. "You mean she d-drinks the moonshine? That stuff is n-nasty."

"Naw," said Big Boy. "She only needs her medicine and a pinch of Brown's Mule chaw to keep her happy. She says he has something else much better."

"What?"

"Search me. Sooner we find out, the quicker we can get back."

"If'n you say s-so. I'll tell you what, I ain't g-going in there. I be staying on Ida in c-case I need to make a quick g-getaway." He poked Ida in the neck, making her bray. "Come on, get a m-move on."

"I'm telling you, Edison, she's gonna get you back if you keep on her like that."

"Only thing lower than c-colored people is a mule. If you can't mess with a m-mule, then you keep it all bottled up."

Big Boy shrugged. "I warned ya, is all I'm saying . . ."

23
Mudtown

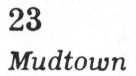

Truman followed Sook's instructions as they approached Mudtown. Nelle seemed to grow more and more nervous the deeper they went into the shantytown.

"Sook, why do you need to make a call in Mudtown? Who do you even know here?" asked Truman, worried about running into Boss. "And, Nelle, what business have you got here?"

Sook stayed focused as they drove slowly past the makeshift houses and surrounding squalor. "Folks been having a mighty tough time the past few years. Even though we're going through our own hard times, most folks out here got it even worse. I been sending Little Bit out with any leftovers we have. She finds women and kids all the time scrounging in the woods for food, living on boiled roots, or once in a blue moon, they might catch a turtle or squirrel and make a stew."

"But you lost your home and everything, Miss Sook," said Nelle. "I don't think you need to help others when you need to help yourself."

"Home is where the heart is, Nelle. Those were just things. Houses can be rebuilt. Stuff bought again," said Sook. "We got family taking us in, so we gonna have a real Christmas even though everything else ain't as it should be. Other folks here don't even have that. Not a tree or present to be seen. Over there, Truman . . ."

She pointed at a rundown shack of a home with cardboard for walls and tin sheets for a roof. Both Nelle and Truman knew it was Boss's house.

Truman skidded to a stop. "Sook, what are we doing *here?*" Panic rose in his voice.

Sook held up her hand. "Now, now, Big Boy told me about the little skirmish you all had with the Henderson boy yesterday. I'm just here to help make peace."

Nelle slunk down in her seat. "Miss Sook, I don't think you know what you're in for. Boss ain't no boy. He's a monster."

"Oh, *pshaw*," she said, waving Nelle off. "Didn't you say that about Sonny Boular before? And he turned out to be okay."

Before they could convince Sook otherwise, she was out of the car and headed for the front door, which was fashioned from an old piece of plywood. "Honey catches more flies than vinegar," she said to no one.

Truman and Nelle exchanged glances; then Nelle opened her door too.

"And where are *you* going?" asked Truman.

"I made a promise to A.C.," she said nobly.

Suddenly, she heard growling. Nelle saw a dog charging and jumped back into the car and shut her door just before it leaped at her. The dog pawed at the window, barking like a rabid beast.

"Or I could wait a little," said Nelle, out of breath.

Sook came back and shooed the dog away. "Go on, git!" she said. The dog scampered off and then sat down the road, watching them.

Sook knocked on the front door. It opened and she spoke to someone, but it was too dark in the shack to see who. Then she went inside.

"They let her in," said Nelle.

Minutes went by that seemed like hours. The dog inched closer. "Maybe Boss got her back for what you did," said Truman.

"What *we* did," said Nelle. Between the dog and her imagination, she couldn't stand the wait. "We can't just sit by and let him get her—"

The front door suddenly swung open and they both shut their eyes tight, fearing the worst.

"What are you two up to?" asked Sook as she climbed back in the car. "Come on, let's go." She tossed a treat to the dog, who gobbled it up and went on its way.

Truman opened one eye and saw her seated next to him. "Well?"

"Well what?" she asked innocently. "I fixed everything. You're welcome."

Nelle popped up cautiously in the back seat. "You mean he's not going to kill us?"

Sook laughed. "Who? Young Peter? He was quite the gentleman. Do you know he plays piano?"

"He played piano for you?" asked Truman.

"Well, they don't *own* a piano, but he showed me, playing on the table, like such." Sook moved her fingers around the dashboard. "Mrs. Henderson, poor woman, was so kind and grateful when I invited him over for Christmas dinner."

"Wait, you *what?*" said Truman.

"You shoulda seen the state of that place. Old Catfish lost his job. Dirt floors, old mattresses on the ground. They couldn't afford a real Christmas if they tried."

"He's coming over—for dinner? At *your* place?" asked Nelle.

"Oh, don't be ridiculous," said Sook. But before they could breathe a sigh of relief, she added, "Our place burned down. He's coming over to Big Boy's. Said he'd even play a song for Truman."

Truman put his head in his hands. "How'd he say it?" he asked.

Sook thought about it. "Oh, something about making you dance till you drop."

Truman gulped. This was not the Christmas he had been hoping for.

Sook turned to Nelle. "Now, dear, who did you need to see?"

Nelle fell back into her seat. "Never mind. I'll figure out another way."

Edison stayed back with the mules while Big Boy inched his way toward Indian Joe's cabin door. Edison was nervous, hiding behind Ida and elbowing her whenever she bumped him aside.

Even though Sook said the rumors weren't true, Big Boy was nervous too. *All those stories can't be wrong*, he thought. He remembered Truman telling him about his and Nelle's encounter with Indian Joe at the snake pits.

He stopped at the cabin door and was about to knock when he noticed something off to the side: a cottonwood tree with dead snakes hanging from its bare branches.

Big Boy's mouth dropped open; his hand froze in midair before he could knock. That was when he heard the scream.

He whipped around and saw the top of Edison's head stuck in Ida's mouth. "Help! Help! My scalp's comin' off!"

Edison was trying to hit Ida's neck, but every time he swung, the mule stepped back, pulling Edison with her.

Big Boy ran over and began tugging on Edison, but the more he pulled, the more that stubborn mule dug in. "My head's c-coming off!" cried Edison.

Big Boy thought the mule really was going to tear Edison's noggin right off. "Let go, Mary!"

Edison held on to his head, screaming. "That's Ida! M-my brain's coming out!"

Big Boy felt someone behind him. He spun around to find

Indian Joe standing there in a fur coat and boots, his leathery skin highlighted by the whites of his glaring eyes. Big Boy almost fainted.

"Can you help him?" Big Boy cried.

Indian Joe reached his hand into the mule's mouth and searched around till he found the animal's tongue. When he grabbed it and pulled it out the side of her mouth, the mule let go.

Edison fell to the ground, mule saliva all over his head. "I'm b-bleeding, I'm bleeding!"

Joe ignored him, released the mule's tongue, and stroked the animal's mane, whispering in her ear. Big Boy bent down and carefully moved Edison's hair around, looking for blood.

"If she wanted to bleed you, she would have bitten your head off," said Indian Joe. "She was trying to teach you a lesson. I saw you from the window."

Joe didn't sound like a real Indian. At least, not like the ones in the movies.

"I think my n-nut is broken . . ." mumbled Edison.

"You'll live," said Joe. "You of all people shouldn't be making life miserable for those below you. Do you like how the white man treats you?"

Big Boy took offense. "We treat him good. Him and his pa work on our farm."

"Do you speak for him?" asked Joe. "Are you his owner?"

Big Boy didn't like this Joe. "Are you even a real Indian? You don't sound like one."

Joe tied the mule to a post and stood up straight with his palm out. "How," he said, deep-voiced, like a movie Indian.

Big Boy raised his hand. "How?"

Joe shook his head. "*How* on earth did you boys get this far in life?" He busted out laughing. "*How*," he said again, "do you do!" And laughed all the way back to the cabin.

Big Boy watched him go inside and shut the door. "Them Indians is strange."

Edison was holding his head as if it might fall apart if he let go. "Ow—I don't th-think he's an Indian . . ."

"How do you know?"

"He were wearing white s-spats over his shoes."

"Oh." Big Boy thought about how he used to pretend to be Inspector Lestrade and figured that Joe's whole Indian act was part of his business image. "If your brains ain't leaking, let's get this over with and go on home."

Edison sat and cradled his head while keeping an eye on Mary and Ida.

Big Boy knocked on the door. He heard Joe say "*How*" again and laugh. The door opened a crack.

"Sook sent us," Big Boy said, peeking in.

"Don't know no Sook," said Joe from the darkness. Big Boy heard a rattling noise, and when Joe stepped into the light, he was holding the largest snake Big Boy had ever seen—head to toe as big as the man himself.

Indian Joe had his hands on the snake's neck, holding its

mouth open so he could see its fangs. "Eastern diamondback. Deadliest snake in Alabama. One bite an' you got about fifteen seconds to live."

Big Boy gulped and thought about running. But his feet wouldn't move.

"Whatchu want, boy? Indian Joe ain't got all day."

"S-sook. F-fruit-c-cakes," he stuttered.

Joe grinned in recognition. "Oh, that ol' fruitcake lady who come around. I know what she wants." He let out a hoarse laugh and started coughing as he disappeared back into the dark.

Once Big Boy's eyes adjusted to the dimness, he noticed that the walls were lined with wooden crates filled with ocher-colored bottles, and on top of those were a bunch of glass fish aquariums, only they were full of snakes.

He hated snakes.

"Here," said Joe, coming back and thrusting a cotton sack at Big Boy.

"What is it?" he asked, dubious.

"It's a surprise." He cackled.

Big Boy had seen handlers carrying snakes around in these very sacks. He poked at it, but it didn't move. He took the bag and peeked inside.

"*Kumquats?* That's her secret? I coulda gone to the store and gotten those!" said Big Boy.

Joe didn't seem offended. "Don't think so, boy. These are Meiwa. Extra-sweet. Brought back seeds from China on Joe's many travels abroad. You won't find these nowhere around here, son. That'll be ten dollars."

"Ten dollars! That's highway robbery." Big Boy eyed him suspiciously. "I bet these are as Chinese as you are Indian!"

Joe grinned and had himself a chuckle. "Tell you what," he said in a true southern Alabama accent. "You tell ol' Sook to give me two of them fruitcakes and we'll call it even. Meanwhile, I'll take this—"

He snatched the five dollars Big Boy was holding in his hand. "Now git before I set Betsy on you!"

He thrust the snake's fangs toward him and Big Boy bolted faster than a jackrabbit being chased by a fox. He ran back to the mules, and he wasn't five feet from Edison before he noticed the two black strangers his friend was talking to.

24
Outsiders

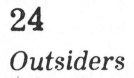

Jenny was not in a good mood. Truman, Sook, Big Boy, and Edison had all disappeared, and so had her car. That added up to no good in her eyes.

Bud was having his morning coffee. "Don't worry none. I taught Tru how to drive a tractor when he was nine. I'm sure he's an old pro at it now."

Jenny stared out the window. "This has to be Sook's doing. I know she can't drive, and only someone with her sensibilities would think of such a thing. We will have words."

That meant one of Jenny's famous tirades. She was already on edge; she just wanted some peace and quiet and hoped to make it through the holidays intact.

Jennings Sr. was having his coffee too when he noticed his

mules making their way back to the farm. He immediately saw Big Boy and Edison sitting on Mary. Then he noticed two dark-skinned men riding Ida behind them.

"What in the . . ."

The adults gathered around the kitchen window as Big Boy and Edison rode up and set the mules back in their stalls. The two strangers waited with Edison while Big Boy ran to the back of the house carrying a sack.

Big Boy was surprised to see everyone waiting for him. "Just where have you been?" asked Jennings Sr. "And who the heck are those men?"

Big Boy wasn't sure which question to answer first. "Um, I was out with Edison getting some ingredients for Sook's fruitcakes, like I promised her." He held open the sack for proof.

"And where are Sook and Truman?" asked Jenny.

Big Boy skirted the question. "As for those men . . . that's Frank and Brown Ezell. They were traveling downriver when their boat started leaking. They're hungry and tired and was just looking for a place to rest up before they hitch a ride back to Mobile."

The adults eyed the two men, who were clearly chilled to the bone and looked like they hadn't slept in ages.

Jennings Sr. sighed. "You know we're already full up, son. Tell them to be on their way."

"That's what I told Edison. But he says he knows them and wants to help. They won't mind spending the night in the barn," said Big Boy. "It's the Christian thing to do."

"Tell Edison to come in here," Jennings Sr. said.

Big Boy turned in the doorway and waved his friend over. Edison ran in, took off his hat, and stared at the floor.

"How do you know these men, Edison?" asked Jennings Sr.

"They father and s-son, sir. They come through few times b-before, selling fish and doing odd j-jobs. Good people. Just on h-hard times, like most."

Jennings mulled it over. "I suppose two more won't make a difference for one night. Can they work?"

Edison nodded.

"Fine, then. Dang mules busted a hole in the side of the wall. Have 'em fix it up, and in exchange I'll give 'em some supper. But they best be gone in the morning, hear?"

Edison smiled and ran out to tell them.

As soon as the back door slammed shut, the front door opened. Everyone turned around to see Truman, Nelle, and Sook.

"You three have a lot of explaining to do," said Jenny sternly. "Why on earth did you steal my car?"

Sook stood in front of Tru and Nelle. "We were on a mission of peace. I had to save the children."

"From what?" asked Jenny.

"From Boss Henderson, that's what!" said Nelle. "He almost killed Truman until I whacked him on the noggin. We thought he was dead until we saw him alive in town, and then Big Boy sent Sook here to negotiate a peace so we wouldn't all die 'cause of some Christmas tree—"

Nelle stopped when she saw the two black strangers talking to Edison outside.

She sucked in her breath. "Who's that?" she asked excitedly.

"Never you mind. Just two folks Big Boy and Edison met down by the river. What I want to know is—"

"Tru—what if that's *them?*"

"Who?" asked Truman.

"The two the sheriff is looking for!" she hissed.

She and Truman went over to the window to get a better look. Jenny was exasperated. "*Why* is the sheriff looking for them?"

Nelle spun around and collected her thoughts. "They might be the men who attacked Mr. Northrup yesterday at the general store."

"Good Lord," said Jenny, sitting down and fanning herself. "I thought my house burning down was enough, but now we're harboring criminals!"

Bud scowled. "Young lady, before you start spreading rumors and speculating on the guilt or innocence of two men, you better be sure of what you're saying."

"Look, one of them is limping," said Nelle.

Truman turned to Bud. "They do fit the profile. They must have come downriver past the general store. And there are two of them."

"One of 'em has a rag with a dark stain on it tied around his hand," said Big Boy. "Could be blood."

Mary Ida couldn't stand it anymore. "I'll not have two

robbers stay on our farm with Christmas coming up. We need to turn them away."

"We mustn't anger them," said Truman carefully. "They killed Mr. Northrup and might be carrying weapons."

"*What?*" all the adults said at once.

"I didn't see none," said Big Boy. "They look poorer than a stick to me. Still, it is mighty strange for them to be headed downriver right now."

"We need to tell A.C. He'll know what to do," said Nelle.

"We need to tell someone, and quick," said Jenny. "I'll take the children. Bud, you and Jennings Sr. keep an eye on them. And for heaven's sake, get Edison away from there."

Mary Ida just shook her head and stared at Truman. "Things were a lot quieter before you showed up, young Truman."

"Mary Ida! Don't say such a thing," said Sook. "Truman is a blessing for us all."

"No," said Truman. "She's right—wherever I go, I make things worse. I don't blame her for wanting me to leave."

"Now you're being silly. She said no such thing. Did you, Mary Ida?" asked Jenny.

Mary Ida was silent for a moment. "No, I said no such thing," she said, smiling weakly. "I'm just tired, is all . . ."

Jenny shook her head. "Come on, children, we're going to Nelle's house until this is settled." She pointed at Truman. "And *you* are not driving."

"Sook made me, Jenny. Honest," said Truman.

Big Boy handed the bag of kumquats to Sook. "This is what you was asking for. How did your meeting go?"

"It were downright pleasant. I don't think you have anything to worry about," said Sook.

"Whew. Thanks for talking some sense into Boss." He eyed the strangers. "At least *he* won't kill us now."

"Well, you can see for yourself when he comes for Christmas dinner," said Sook. She popped one of the kumquats into her mouth. "Mmm, just right!"

Big Boy took a step toward the door and stopped. "Wait—Boss is coming *here* for Christmas?"

Sook nodded. "'Tis the season," she said as she tried another kumquat.

Edison watched as Jenny's car drove off. "Where they going?" asked Frank.

"D-don't know . . ." Edison said.

Frank's son, Brown, was nervous and worn out, which made him look older than his twenty years. "You got a phone in the house?" he asked.

"No, s-sir. No 'lectricity or runnin' water yet. This ain't M-Monroeville, you know." Edison glanced at the rag tied around Frank's hand. "You c-cut yourself? Need a fresh d-dressing?"

Frank's nappy hair was graying and slightly wild. His eyes were resigned to some fate Edison couldn't understand. "Cut myself skinning a fish," he answered, even though it wasn't exactly fishing season.

Edison saw Bud and Jennings Sr. coming out of the house. "Oh, here comes B-Big Boy's daddy and his uncle B-Bud. They'll set you up in the b-barn, I s'pose. I slept in there once. C-cows keep it warm."

The strangers looked warily at Jennings Sr. and Bud. Bud was carrying a jug and a plate covered with a towel. Jennings had a rifle with him.

"Boys," said Bud. "Brought you something to eat." He handed the plate to the older man, who'd removed his hat politely. Bud noticed that their clothing had some dark stains on it.

"Much obliged, sirs. Thank yas. I'm Frank, and this here my boy, Brown."

Bud nodded. "Big Boy said you was having trouble navigating the river. Something about a boat leak?"

"Yassir. Looking to find some work up here going toward Selma. Thought we could fish along the way. Bass and whatnot."

"Bass is good eatin', that's for sure," said Bud. "Kind of late in the season, though."

"Yassir. But we wasn't expecting this freeze. Ain't never seen it this cold, to be honest," said the man.

"You can say that again," said Jennings. "Almost froze all my crops. Gonna set me back some, I can tell you that."

The young man looked at Bud's rifle. "If we putting you out too much, we can be on our way—"

"No, no. It's fine," said Jennings Sr. "Help out a family in need, even if our accommodations aren't the best, I always say. You'll find some horse blankets in the barn and plenty of hay to make a bed with. We'll bring you some more vittles come nightfall."

They stood there awkwardly for a few moments. "Say, Edison, I have something for you at the house," said Bud.

Edison tilted his head. "What's that, Mr. B-Bud?"

Bud hadn't thought that far ahead. "Um, need some help with the Christmas decorations. You know how Sook likes to get everything in order before the big day."

"We can help if you like," the older man offered.

"No, no, Edison will be enough. Thank you. You fellas just settle in. Okey-dokey?"

The men nodded.

"Come on, Edison, we, uh, got work to do," said Bud unconvincingly.

25
Sheriff Makes a Move

While Jenny looked on nervously, A.C. listened to Nelle and Truman present their case. They'd talked and conjectured the whole way over, making Jenny more and more upset.

"I wish you all wouldn't let your minds run wild like that," she said.

"It's science," Truman said. "Or deduction, as Sherlock Holmes would say."

"I'd say it's nosy," said Jenny.

Nelle paced back and forth, describing what she'd seen and heard. "I mean, the sheriff's gotta look into it, right? We can't leave the rest of Tru's family out there alone," she said.

"I'm not worried about Jennings Sr. and Bud. They can handle themselves," said A.C. "But if what you say is true, the sheriff will get on it. I just don't like the idea of you getting involved in this mess, Nelle. I told you, this isn't some kind of game. I thought you both were over that kind of thing."

Truman shrugged, looking at his shoes. "We're just trying to help . . ."

"Well, let me put in a call." A.C. used the phone in the hall. He was patched through to the sheriff and started to explain what was going on. Halfway through telling the story, A.C. stopped talking and hung up the receiver. "Looks like you've got your wish. He said he and his deputy were on their way."

Nelle looked excitedly at Tru, then back to A.C. "Well? What're we waiting for?"

A.C. sat down and took out his pipe. "If you think we are going to rush back to the farm to watch, you've got another think coming. We're waiting *here*."

Nelle's shoulders slumped. "Aww . . ."

Jenny sat down as well. "I don't know why I didn't insist Mary Ida and Sook come too. The thought of them up there alone with those —"

"Presumed innocent men," said A.C. as he lit his pipe.

"Of course, Mr. Lee," she said. "Still . . ."

Nelle motioned Truman over to the hallway. He followed while Jenny and A.C. talked. "Do you think they done the deed?" asked Nelle.

"Hard to say," said Truman. "We haven't had time to investigate. And I'm not sure I really want to."

Jennings Sr., Bud, and Mary Ida hid behind the kitchen counter as they watched the barn. Jennings Sr. had his rifle at the ready. Mary Ida kept eyeing her butcher's knife, just in case. The strangers had gone inside, and nothing appeared to be out of the ordinary. The sky was getting darker and the temperature was dropping even further.

Edison and Sook were at the kitchen table, stringing popcorn for Christmas decorations. "Do you help your father with the decorations at home?" Sook asked.

Edison poked himself with the needle as he threaded some corn. "D-don't really have much to d-decorate in that shack. Ever since M-Mama passed, we ain't been m-much for C-Christmas. Daddy always saying that the n-new year might b-bring about a new start. B-but I don't s-see it."

"Hmm, maybe Santa will still find you out in that field," said Sook.

Edison laughed. "Miss Sook, S-Santa don't visit c-colored folk."

Sook stopped stringing popcorn and touched Edison on the arm. "Well, you never know." She winked. "I'll put in a good word."

"They're coming!" said Bud.

He pointed at the sheriff's black car whipping down the

main road. It passed the house and skidded to a stop in front of the barn. Sheriff Farrish and a deputy jumped out, guns drawn.

"Oh my," said Mary Ida. "I do hope they don't hurt those men."

Edison went to the window and saw the sheriff and his partner creep up on the main door. Edison's eyes grew wide. "They gonna sh-shoot 'em."

The sheriff jumped through the barn door and a few seconds passed with no sounds. Then Edison spotted the younger man, Brown, crawling out the barn's hayloft and dropping to the ground. Brown hesitated and then began to limp quickly away.

Toward them.

Everybody gasped. Edison jumped up and headed for the door. "Edison, no!" said Mary Ida as she grabbed for him, but he managed to slip onto the porch.

His heart raced as he headed toward Brown. Edison thought about showing him the way through the forest. When he saw the deputy pop out of the hayloft too, then draw his weapon, Edison panicked and sped out to intervene. "N-no!"

A warning shot was fired into the air. Brown stopped in his tracks and raised his hands. Edison ran up to him and stood between him and the deputy, who was closing in fast.

Brown was out of breath. "We didn't do nothing. Honest. We just stopped at the store for supplies, but the man was already on the ground bleeding. Pa was trying to help him, but I knew if anyone saw us, they'd think we done it. Pa would never hurt a fly!"

Edison looked into the young man's pleading eyes. In that moment, he believed him.

The deputy pushed Edison aside and tackled Brown to the frozen ground. Brown didn't put up a fight, but the deputy still shouted, "Don't move!" Then he realized he'd dropped his gun. He scrambled off the young man, snatched up his weapon, and pointed it in Brown's face as if he were trying to escape. "Don't even think it, heathen!"

The deputy's hand was shaking. Edison thought he might accidentally shoot him. He took a step toward the deputy to try and calm his nerves, but the deputy spun around and pointed his gun at Edison.

"He didn't d-do it!" Edison said.

Jennings Sr. came running out. "Don't shoot! He works for us!"

The deputy's gaze jumped from Jennings Sr. to Edison and back to Brown. He finally settled on pointing his gun at Brown.

"I got him!" he shouted to the sheriff, who was pushing Frank out of the barn.

"He didn't d-do it," Edison said again.

"Guilty men don't run," said the deputy, a big grin on his face. "I got you!" He poked Brown with the barrel of his gun.

Edison tried to reason with him. "He was s-scared—"

"Who's talking to you, boy?" said the deputy. "Maybe I'll arrest you too. Aiding and abetting—"

Jennings Sr. intervened. "Now, now, let's just take a breath. Edison's a good boy."

The deputy looked at Jennings Sr., then at Edison. "Boy should learn his place, then."

The suspects were handcuffed and put into the sheriff's car, where the deputy kept his beady eyes trained on them.

The sheriff strutted over to Jennings Sr. and shook his hand. "You're a lucky one."

"How's that, Sheriff?"

He glanced back at the car. "They could've gone after your whole family. Ruined a perfectly good Christmas."

"They seemed harmless enough."

Sherriff spat onto the ground. "Tell that to Bill Northrup. I think he'd disagree." He cast an eye on Edison. "You the one that brought 'em here?"

Edison nodded.

"If you was white, I'd give you a reward," said the sheriff. "But seeing as you ain't, you're lucky they didn't—"

"That's enough, Sheriff," said Jennings Sr. "You can go now."

Jennings Sr. and the rest watched the sheriff get into his car and drive out onto the slushy road.

"Never you mind them, Edison," said Jennings Sr.

"Y-yes, sir."

He put a hand on the boy's neck. "Just do me a favor."

Edison looked him in the eye as Jennings Sr. tightened his grip. "Don't you ever bring a stranger onto our farm again or you and your daddy will be on the outside of things, hear?"

Edison heard.

26
Wrong Man for the Job

Night descended, and winter settled in for the long haul. A.C. stayed at home instead of going to the jail, taking calls and speaking in hushed tones. Nelle tried to find out more, but A.C. kicked her out of his study.

Her mother was on edge too, talking to herself and occasionally shouting something out the window at a passerby. "Don't walk so fast or you'll slip and kill yourself!"

Nelle settled down and did crossword puzzles with her mother, which tended to calm her nerves. She was incredibly sharp when she focused, and her way with words was one talent she'd passed on to Nelle.

Word was spreading around town that the two killers had

been apprehended. Most of the rumors were due to the sheriff bragging outside the town jail.

Jenny was pacing in Nelle's kitchen, upset and full of doubts. Truman tried to ease her mind.

"You don't have to worry. They're locked up now," said Truman.

"But what if they have the wrong men?" asked Jenny. "The killers could still be out there . . ."

"Well, the chances of two sets of killers wandering onto the farm is unlikely. But if you like, me and Big Boy could stay the night here."

Big Boy wasn't too keen on spending the night with Nelle and her family. "Truman's right. Sheriff got the right men. It's all good . . ."

"I suppose," said Jenny. "But perhaps you two should stay here for the night. Let me go back and make sure everything is okay."

Truman agreed and cut off Big Boy before he could talk her out of it. "That's right, go on home. We'll be fine here."

Truman and Big Boy watched Jenny from the driveway as she drove back to the farm without looking at the remains of her old house.

"What'd ya do that for?" asked Big Boy when she was out of sight.

Truman put his hands on Big Boy's shoulders. "Aren't you curious?"

"About what?"

Truman didn't answer. He was staring at a man standing on Nelle's front porch knocking.

It was Judge Fountain.

"About that. Come on." He pulled Big Boy down the side of the house as A.C. answered the door. From the back door, they snuck into the parlor and found Nelle finishing up a crossword puzzle for her mother, who was sound asleep on the sofa.

Truman held his finger to his lips and motioned for her to follow. She dropped the paper and they tiptoed into the hallway, where they could hear voices coming from the study.

They turned into the dining room and knelt down by the vent to eavesdrop.

They could hear A.C. pacing. "I don't know, Judge. Due process allows a man—"

"Due process! There's talk of a mob forming. If we don't move quickly, justice will be served without us."

A.C. hesitated. "I'm not a criminal lawyer. Not for this kind of case, anyway. Hank Greenspan would be much better—"

"People trust you, Mr. Lee. You're a community man who's worked his way up from nothing and now has a finger in every pie in town, from the newspaper to the chamber of commerce to the church. People see you up there defending these men, they'll know it's because you're applying the letter of the law. When the jury finds them guilty, no one will be able to complain."

There was a long moment of silence. Truman looked at Nelle and Big Boy, who were waiting for A.C.'s answer. Finally, A.C. spoke.

"If I represent these men, it'll be because it's their right to have proper counsel."

The judge spoke like he might to a child. "Of course, Mr. Lee. I wouldn't want it any other way."

A.C. was tapping his penknife on his desk. "Very well. When were you thinking? After the new year?"

"No, no, man. Have you not heard what I've been saying? Time is of the essence. We'll go up tomorrow. People will likely be calmer during the annual lighting of the tree in the town square. We'll do it quick, before Catfish and his boys get any momentum."

"Tomorrow? Judge, I must object. These men—"

"Overruled, Counselor, but your protest is duly noted. You may interview the defendants tonight. In fact, you might want to stay there, just in case things get out of hand. Then I want you in the courthouse at ten a.m."

"But—"

"Good night, Amasa."

They heard the judge walk down the hallway and out the door. The silence that followed was deafening. Nelle, Truman, and Big Boy moved toward the study and peeked in.

A.C. was seated at his desk, slumped in his wooden chair. He didn't even look up. Truman glanced at Nelle, but her brow was furrowed; she was lost in thought. Finally, she left the boys and padded over to A.C. She put her hand on his arm and, when he didn't notice, rested her head on his shoulder. The boys dipped back into the shadows.

"Word," she said. "*W* and seven."

He exhaled and patted her hand. *"Worried,"* he answered.

She waited for more but he wasn't talking. "What're you gonna do, A.C.?" she asked.

He blinked, then acknowledged her presence by holding her hand. "I'll do what I can, Nelle. It's all I can do."

"But it's Christmas. Can't justice wait?"

He looked at her for the first time. "No. Justice can wait for no man. I have a duty to perform. Thank you for reminding me." He noticed Truman and Big Boy lingering in the shadows.

"You two keep an eye on my daughter, will you? I have to go to work." He stood up and walked to the doorway. "And under no circumstances are you to follow me, hear? This is for grownups only."

All three nodded. Truman had his fingers crossed. "Yes, sir."

After he left, Truman turned to Nelle. "Well?"

"Well what? You heard him," she said.

"Silly, can't you read between the lines? He wants us to come," said Truman.

"I didn't hear nothing between them lines, Truman," said Big Boy. "And I've had enough trouble to last me all winter."

"Me too," said Nelle. "I can't lie to A.C. Besides, I gotta stay here with Mama."

Truman made a face. "You're no fun anymore. Maybe Big Boy was right not to include you in the boys' club."

"Who said I wanted to be in your stupid boys' club?" said Nelle.

"You don't?" Big Boy acted surprised. "Maybe we got bigger things to worry about than A.C.'s business."

"Like?" asked Truman.

"Like Boss coming over to the farm for Christmas?"

In all the excitement, Truman had forgotten.

Nelle laughed. "You should see the look on your face."

"What am I gonna do?" Tru asked.

"What do you mean, *you?* What am *I* gonna do?" said Big Boy. "You don't think he'll really show up, do you? I mean, I don't imagine he'd want to have supper with the likes of us."

Tru's face brightened. "Maybe you're right. Just because Sook invited him doesn't mean he'll show. And if he *does* show, he can't kill us because his mama would hear about it."

"You realize that don't make a lick of sense," said Nelle.

Truman sighed. He knew.

27

The Getaway

Truman woke to the sound of voices and automobiles. He and Big Boy had fallen asleep in Nelle's sisters' old room. When the flash of a car headlight settled on his face, Truman sat up. It was the middle of the night and he could see his breath in the room, as the wood stove had gone out. He crept to the window that overlooked the main road and saw something he hadn't seen since his Halloween party a few years back.

Men dressed in white robes and pointy hats.

Never a good sign. He shook Big Boy, who popped up. "What's wrong?" He saw it before Truman could point it out.

"They're on their way to the jailhouse," whispered Truman. "Let's get Nelle."

They crept into the hall and pressed their ears against Nelle's door. Truman could hear gentle snores. He pushed on the door—it creaked—but he steadied it and opened it enough to sneak in.

They were surprised to see Nelle's mother asleep on the extra bed. She was snoring louder. They snuck over to Nelle's bed and Truman put his hand over her mouth. She jumped up with a start and slugged Truman in the arm before she realized it was him.

"Ow! Stop!" he hissed. "Get up. Something's going on."

"Oh," said Big Boy. "Look!"

He was pointing out the window at A.C.'s car, which had pulled up behind the house without the headlights on. The sheriff slowly emerged from the passenger side with his gun drawn. A.C. came out from his side and walked quickly to the cellar door. He jangled his keys while the sheriff waited impatiently, then unlocked the door.

The sheriff opened the car's back door and stood watch as the two Ezell men slowly came out. They looked terrified and were quickly hustled into the basement.

"What on earth—" whispered Nelle. "Why would they bring them *here?*"

"Probably to escape that mob that's forming at the jailhouse. Lots of people liked Mr. Northrup. Especially people in the Klan . . ."

"Why, that's just about the dumbest thing—if Mama finds out, she'll lose it for sure. The whole town will know," said Nelle.

Of course they had to find out what was going on.

The Getaway

Nelle threw on her overalls and grabbed a flashlight from her dresser. They snuck out of the room without waking her mother. Nelle made her way to the kitchen and waved them toward an old dumbwaiter that connected to the cellar.

They could hear muffled voices, then footsteps, and the sheriff came out of the cellar, shut the door tight, and locked it. Big Boy peeked out the window and saw the sheriff pause like he knew this was a bad idea, but then he shook his head and hustled away on foot.

Truman put his ear to the dumbwaiter floor. "I can't hear anything," said Truman. "Does this thing go down into the cellar?"

"Of course," she answered. "It's one of them dummy-waiters for bringing stuff up."

Suddenly, they heard footsteps coming up the basement stairs *inside* the house. The door to the hallway opened and A.C. wearily stepped out. He locked that door and rattled its handle to make sure it wouldn't turn.

Next thing they knew, he came into the kitchen. They froze in the dark, not saying a word or moving a muscle. A.C. didn't notice them. He just grabbed one of the chairs and took it out into the hallway.

The front door opened and closed again. Nelle peeked out of the kitchen.

"What's he doing?" asked Big Boy.

"He's sitting in front of the door on the porch. Like he's guarding the house."

"Does he have a gun?" Truman asked.

"A.C. don't believe in guns," she said, matter-of-fact. "If that mob comes here, he'll deal with them in his own way."

Truman had seen him do it before. But this time, the crowd would be wanting blood.

The dumbwaiter suddenly moved. Someone was tugging on the line.

"Um, Nelle . . ." Big Boy was pointing at the dumbwaiter.

"They're trying to escape!" said Truman.

"Don't be loony," said Nelle. "They couldn't escape up that little box. Why, the only one who could fit in there might be Truman."

She walked over to the tiny elevator-like contraption and stuck her head in the box, put her ear to the floor.

"Psst," someone said.

Nelle jerked up and banged her head on the top of the dumb-waiter. "They're trying to talk to us," she said, rubbing her head.

"You sure they can't escape?" asked Big Boy. Nelle shook her head. So Big Boy walked past her and pulled the dumbwaiter a few feet up so he could stick his head underneath and look down the shaft.

Brown Ezell was looking back at him. "Is it you?" he asked quietly, holding up a candle.

Big Boy puzzled over the question. Of course it was him. Who else would he be? "What do you want?" he whispered back.

"Can you help us?" Brown asked.

Big Boy turned to Nelle. "He wants help."

Nelle poked her head in and looked down. She had so much she wanted to say, but all that came out was "Did you do it?"

Brown looked back at her, weary and beaten down. "We didn't do nothing, miss."

"How can we know that for sure?" she asked.

Brown's eyes pleaded with her. "Miss, we just workers who go from place to place. The boy Edison knows us. We got no reason to kill nobody."

He didn't seem like a killer to Nelle, but then again, she'd never met one. She reached into the front pocket of her overalls and felt the small plastic Santa she'd found over at Murder Creek. She pulled it out and held it over the shaft.

"Is this yours?" she asked.

Brown squinted. "What that be? Can't see it from down here."

She turned her flashlight on it. "It's a little plastic Santa I found in the dirt outside the riverfront store."

His eyes went wide in recognition.

"You took it from the store?" she asked.

He shook his head. "I bought it for my mama. I ain't no thief. Fell out of my pocket when I slipped in the mud."

Nelle wasn't sure she believed him. She put the Santa back in her pocket. "A.C.'s a good man. If you're innocent, he'll have you out and back home for Christmas, I'm sure of it."

Brown breathed out slowly. "He seem like the only one looking out for us. But, miss, you're a young'un who ain't seen much of this world. I don't think we'll get out of this alive."

Nelle gasped and pulled out.

"What?" asked Truman. Nelle couldn't talk.

Truman stuck his head into the shaft. "You're saying you didn't do it?" he asked.

"I am."

"You'd swear on the Holy Bible to that?" Truman asked.

"Yes, sir," he answered.

"Well, there you go. Folks in Monroeville are God-fearing people. You swear on the Good Book and no harm will come to you," said Truman.

That seemed like a good answer.

Brown didn't say anything more and vanished into the darkness.

"What's happening?" asked Big Boy.

"I don't know. He disappeared," said Truman.

Frank's head came into view as he struggled to look up the shaft. "Young mister?"

"Yes?" said Truman.

"We haven't eaten since they took us. Might we have some food?" the older man asked.

Truman turned to Nelle. "They're hungry. Can you get something for them to eat?"

"We ain't got much," said Nelle. "But let me get some bread and jam and maybe some ham together."

"I'll help too," said Big Boy. Nelle paused, then nodded.

Truman turned back to the shaft. "Food's coming. Is there anything else we can do?"

Frank massaged his neck. "Well, I'd really like to send word to my wife so she knows where we are. I don't want her to worry about that mob, but if she could get the preacher and her sisters here, it might help."

"Have you asked A.C.?"

"Yassir. But he said no one can drive out this time of night."

Truman sighed. "I'm not allowed to drive anymore," he said. "You best wait till morning." Truman was about to pull out when the man spoke one last time.

"But what if morning never come?"

28
Lighting the Tree

Truman, Big Boy, and Nelle didn't sleep much the rest of the night. They could hear A.C. pacing back and forth on the porch till the darkness grew into a gray winter's morning. Then the pacing finally stopped.

By the time they went downstairs to see what was happening, A.C. and his prisoners were gone. The sheriff must have come and gotten them, as there were no signs of trouble.

"A.C. went to work," said Brother. "I'm supposed to keep you here until the unveiling of the town tree at noon."

"But what about the trial?" asked Big Boy.

Brother knew of no trial. Mother came in, humming a Christmas carol—a strange concoction of "Jingle Bells" and

"Hark! The Herald Angels Sing." She was in a good mood, even after seeing Truman and Big Boy there.

"Truman? How is your dear mother and her Cuban?" she asked.

Truman had managed not to think of them in all the excitement. "They were fine the last time I saw them."

"Good, good," she said. "Now, where's my crossword?"

They ate breakfast and sat around nervously all morning. Nelle and Brother had their chores to attend to, leaving Truman and Big Boy to their own devices.

"I sure would like to get down to the courthouse . . ." said Truman.

"Let sleeping dogs lie, Truman. It's two days before Christmas. Might as well try to get in the spirit of things before Boss ruins it."

But Truman didn't want to think about that. He was thinking about a Christmas tree, all right, but it wasn't the one they'd fought Boss over. It was the twenty-footer in the town square.

Truman bided his time until he heard the old clock tower clang eleven thirty. He looked out the front door and saw some of the townspeople starting to make their way to the square. Even Blind Captain Wash and his crippled wife were going.

"Do you smell that?" asked Brother. Nelle sniffed and let the cold drift through her nostrils and into her throat. It smelled like woolen mittens. The air was heavy and still, like it was trapped in by the clouds overhead. "Snow," he said. "I think we're gonna see some today. Wouldn't that be something? A white Christmas in Monroeville!"

Nelle and Brother, Tru, Big Boy, and Mother made their way toward the town square. The town players, a collection of retired farmers and a former Rebel or two, played their brass instruments and banjos while members of the Methodist church choir sang Christmas tunes. It was a bitter cold day, dark clouds hanging low over the proceedings. People were bundled up from head to toe and stood around a handful of fires burning in metal trashcans. Kids looked to the sky, ready for the snow they'd heard was coming. Most had never seen snow before, so the anticipation of snowball fights and building snowmen was the main topic of discussion. In the middle of it all, a giant cone stood twenty feet tall under a tarp. The mood was festive but restless. People knew something was happening in the courthouse but chose not to discuss it.

Walking around, Truman and Nelle heard rumors of men being called in to serve on the jury all morning. Those who were turned away said little. Mr. Northrup had not been a citizen of Monroeville proper, but those who earned their livelihood from the river had known him well.

Truman spotted Boss; his dad, Catfish; and many of Catfish's men milling around their own fire. Truman had a hunch they were the ones who had marched on the jail the night before. If they'd had their way, these men might have overtaken the jailer and dragged the prisoners into the woods, where they'd have met their demise.

"Don't start nothing, Tru. It ain't worth it," said Nelle.

"Boss won't do anything. Not in this crowd," said Truman. "But if you really want to stay out of his way, I know where we can go."

He pointed at the courthouse.

"Forget it. You heard what A.C. said. We're gonna stay here and watch the tree get unveiled and that's that."

"Well, he may be your daddy, but he's not mine. Nor Big Boy's. We can do what we please," said Truman. "And Boss can't stop us."

"Wait—Boss is *here?*" said Big Boy, poking his head up over the crowd. Then he spotted him. "Holy cow! He *is* here!"

Big Boy said it a little too loudly. Boss happened to glance over and saw the three of them looking at him. He chuckled deviously. But then he waved like they were friends.

"I think he's even scarier like that," said Big Boy. "That's how the devil smiles at you."

Truman waved back. "Maybe. But at least he isn't trying to squash my head."

"Ten minutes!" someone announced from the stage. "Ten minutes till the unveiling!"

Truman looked at them both. "Come on, you two. Quit dilly-dallying. Let's go into the courthouse and see what's going on." Nelle and Big Boy glanced at each other, unsure. "Fine," said Truman. "I'll go by myself." He spun on his heel and headed toward the courthouse steps.

He ignored Boss, but out of the corner of his eye, he could see him watching. Truman tried to act casual, like he was just going for a walk. He went up to the first entrance and saw the deputy standing there. Truman thought quickly as he climbed up the steps.

"Where you going, sonny?" the deputy asked.

"Gotta go to the bathroom," he said, acting antsy.

"Courthouse's closed. Try the drugstore."

"But I gotta go *bad!*" said Truman, dancing about.

The deputy didn't care. "Plenty of trees here. Help yourself." He took a step toward Truman, who turned and ran down the stairs.

When the deputy wasn't looking, Truman headed around back, where he knew there was another door. But that one was locked.

"If you want to get in, you'll have to go through the storage window. The lock on that's been busted for years."

Truman turned around and saw Nelle with Big Boy standing behind her. He smiled. "Lead the way."

The storage window was hidden by a host of bushes. It was unlocked, just as Nelle had said. Since he was the tallest, Big Boy boosted her and Truman up, then scrambled in after them.

They came out into a hallway leading toward the stairs to the second floor, where the courtroom was. The building seemed empty. They crept up silently, staying low, till they could peek over the top step.

There were the double doors leading into the courtroom. But a guard stood before them; his back was turned because he was looking through the tiny window in the door.

Truman scanned the hall. His eyes came to rest on the small stairway that led up to the balcony. He pointed over to the staircase. Big Boy pointed at the guard, but Truman just rolled his eyes.

He took off his shoes and gestured for the others to do the same. Then they waited.

When the clock in the tower started chiming noon, they stepped out and quickly made their way to the opposite stairwell, keeping an eye on the guard. Big Boy slipped in his socks but Nelle caught him and together they made it across. They climbed the darkened stairwell and came out on top, next to a window overlooking the square.

There they could see the mayor talking and pointing to the tree. "Come on," whispered Truman.

Big Boy waited for the tree to be unveiled. When it was—a big, bushy twenty-footer already decorated with bulbs that lit up in all colors—he smiled. "Ain't that a sight."

The trio pushed their way through the door marked Coloreds Only and emerged onto the balcony.

The courtroom smelled the way Truman remembered, reeking of tobacco, cheap hair oil, and sweat. They slid into the first row, which carried a different smell: hints of peppermint and the talcum that the black women wore when they came dressed in their Sunday best. It was strange to see the balcony empty.

"Your Honor, I object!" said A.C., his voice echoing around the wooden courtroom.

They poked their heads above the railing and saw A.C. standing behind a table where the defendants, Frank and Brown, were. An all-white jury sat impassively while Judge Fountain, sitting behind the bench, spat into a spittoon.

"Mr. Lee, this is your fifth objection in a row. What is it now?"

A.C. stepped out and pointed to the only young man on the jury. "Your Honor, my clients simply cannot gain any justice when the victim's own *son* sits on this jury!"

Judge Fountain stared at the young man. "I've known this juror since he was a pup. I know him to be decent, honest, and hard-working. I see no reason why he cannot serve."

"Your Honor—"

Judge Fountain banged his gavel. "Mr. Lee, I suggest you spend what little time you have here presenting your case and not worrying about these minor trivialities."

A.C. heaved a sigh, then sat down to confer with his clients. The prosecutor puffed on his cigar as he approached the jurors.

"Gentlemen, we all knew Mr. Northrup to be a fine, upstanding citizen of Monroe County. He served as an integral part of the river community, providing for the needs of fishermen, delivery people, and boaters alike. Even though he'd lost an arm in a sawmill accident, that didn't stop him from working diligently for over thirty years. The county would first like to offer its condolences to Mr. Northrup's son—"

"Your Honor, this is highly unorthodox—" said A.C.

"Mr. Lee, you are trying my patience. Cannot a man offer another man a heartfelt condolence on the loss of his father?"

Nelle wasn't used to seeing her father so helpless. He'd always been a respected member of the town. But today, the judge was ignoring him.

Truman saw that they were not alone up in the balcony. On the other side was a colored man Truman had seen before—the courthouse janitor. He just shook his head and walked back to the exit. He spotted Nelle and removed his hat. "Your father's a good man," he whispered, "but there'll be no justice today."

29
Lost

A.C. had never lost a case so quickly. In the all-white jury's eyes, Frank and Brown Ezell were guilty no matter what A.C. said. It didn't matter that they were upstanding members of the Negro community, that they'd never been arrested, that they were churchgoing folks trying to survive the Great Depression like everyone else, or even that they were guilty only of being in the wrong place at the wrong time. A.C. was given only fifteen minutes to present what case he had, and the jurors returned after barely ten minutes to render their verdict.

"Guilty," the foreman said, to the satisfaction of Judge Fountain.

"Justice has been served," said the judge. "A jury of your peers has found you guilty of this devious crime. As circuit judge of Monroe County, it is my duty to provide the swift and fitting punishment such a crime deserves. I do hereby sentence Frank Ezell and Brown Ezell to hang. May God have mercy on your souls."

The judge rapped his gavel as A.C. whispered to the stunned father and son with a hand on each man's shoulder. Young Brown had panic in his eyes, while his father just stared at his wrists as they were being handcuffed.

Tru, Nelle, and Big Boy couldn't believe it. They sat, their mouths open in shock. "What have I done?" said Nelle.

"You didn't do anything we wouldn't have done too. You only did what you thought was right."

"If it wasn't for me . . ." Nelle said, watching through moist eyes as the Ezells were led out the back door of the courtroom.

Brown had tears running down his cheeks and suddenly grabbed the banister of the jury box and wouldn't let go. "We didn't do nothing!" he shouted to the stunned jurors before the guards wrestled him into the back hallway.

A.C. stood lost in thought. The judge rose and went over to shake his hand. "You must remember that it's up to us to keep these matters in check. Otherwise, the next thing you know, they'll be in our schools and churches and mingling with our children. Is that what you want? I hope you truly know the answer to that, Mr. Lee."

Judge Fountain patted him on the back and followed the crowd out. The jurors lit up cigars and shuffled out a side door. No one seemed particularly troubled by the whole affair.

Nelle couldn't take it anymore. She ran out of the balcony. Truman started after her, but Big Boy held him back. "Let her go," he said.

She raced down the wooden stairs, and a moment later, she came running into the courtroom, where she collided with A.C. and wrapped her arms around his waist.

Truman had never seen A.C. so affected. Normally, nothing seemed to shake his quiet and unassuming demeanor. But now he turned and held his daughter tight. He didn't admonish her for disobeying him.

After a few seconds of watching, Truman pulled on Big Boy's arm. "Come on, let's go."

Outside seemed like a different world. Music played, people danced, and kids raced around. Boss's father and his men seemed to have heard the news and were whooping it up, celebrating a victory.

Big Boy and Truman made their way down the road toward Nelle's house. Big Boy paused for a moment and looked at the sky.

"What is it?" asked Truman.

"Do you hear that?"

Truman looked up. The white of the clouds seemed to be coming down on them. And then something hit him smack in the forehead.

"Ow!" He looked down to see a dime-size ball of ice at his feet. "Hail?"

It came slowly at first; then a shower of golf ball–size chunks of ice fell from the skies, sending everyone scurrying for shelter.

"Run!" said Big Boy. They put their arms over their heads and raced toward Nelle's. But the hail came fast and furious, and they had to quickly duck for cover under the pecan trees that hung over the fence of an old rundown house a hundred feet from Nelle's.

Inside the courthouse, Nelle could hear the strange pinging of hail hitting the roof. She was sitting in the chair her father had occupied, waiting as he gathered his papers together. He stopped when he noticed a list that Brown had scratched out on a piece of scrap paper. Brown couldn't spell well, and to most anyone else, it might've looked like gibberish from a child. But A.C. saw it for what it was: a wish list for Christmas.

The last item said *kandee fur Moma*.

He stared at it for a good minute, folded it up, and put it in his jacket pocket. Then he gazed around him as if he were memorizing the room.

"What're you looking for, A.C.?"

"This was my first and last capital-crime case. And nobody saw it."

Nelle put her hand in his. "I saw it, Daddy," she said. He nodded and she led him down the center aisle to go home.

When they got to the doorway, the hail stopped, leaving a

layer of ice balls littering the sidewalks and roads. A.C. was in too much of a stupor to notice or care.

Before going home, though, A.C. had a couple of stops he needed to make. They walked across the street to Meyer Katz's department store. Outside stood a small black child dressed in a white elf suit, ringing a bell. He stopped when he saw A.C. and Nelle approach and just stood there staring at his white shoes as they passed.

Mr. Katz was a Russian Jew who, rumor had it, sold sheets to the Klan. He was fond of saying "The only free cheese is in the mousetrap." When he saw A.C. heading toward the fine-candy section, he went behind the counter to help A.C. himself.

"Something for the missus?" he said in his thick Eastern European accent. As usual, A.C. had failed to even think about Christmas and what, if any, presents he might afford in these tight times. He didn't answer.

Mr. Katz's eyes scanned his selection of chocolates from all over the country. "Ah, I have the perfect gift for her," he said. He pulled out a collection of heart-shaped confectionery from Chicago nestled in mistletoe.

A.C. gazed absent-mindedly at them and nodded. "And I need something more, well—personal."

Mr. Katz, who had seen much tragedy in his life, recognized pain when he saw it. "Of course," he said quietly. He knew of the trial, and even though he hadn't heard its verdict, he'd assumed the outcome.

He went into the back and returned with a small bouquet of roses made entirely of chocolate and wrapped in a tasteful red bow. When A.C. reached into his pocket for his wallet, Mr. Katz handed him the roses, brushed his hands twice, and held them out as if to say *It's on the house*. Then he stepped away.

A.C. and Nelle walked back to the car in silence. Nelle carried the roses.

When they reached the car, Catfish Henderson was standing there with his son, Boss, leaning on it as if it were theirs. A.C. spotted them but didn't miss a step. In fact, he sped up.

Catfish kept his eyes glued on A.C. while Boss stared down Nelle. She knew A.C. wouldn't be scared and neither would she.

A.C. came right up to them, and Catfish and Boss moved aside. A.C. held the door open for Nelle, who avoided Boss's stare. She quickly got in, and he closed the door behind her.

When he turned, Catfish blocked his way. "Funny how things come around, Mr. Counselor. You always stepping into other people's business, but sometimes it steps on you."

A.C. glared at him, and for a moment Nelle thought her father might strike the man. But his rage quietly subsided and he walked around Catfish and his son, climbed into the car, and drove away.

Because of the hailstorm, most of the crowd had dispersed. The people who had returned either avoided A.C.'s eyes or stared daggers at him.

When he pulled up to their house, he stopped the car but

kept the engine running. He saw that Nelle wasn't going to get out, so he patted her on the knee and resumed driving.

"Why do they hate you, A.C.?" she asked.

He thought about it and said, "They don't hate. They just don't know better. It's the way things are down here."

They drove in silence, slowly leaving Monroeville proper and heading out past Frisco City and Uriah to the main highway. When they reached the swamplands outside Mobile, A.C. turned onto a dirt road leading to a wisp of a town called Creola.

For at least ten minutes, Nelle felt like A.C. was going to say something. Finally, he cleared his throat and said, "When I was seventeen, I got a job carrying mail by horseback. Did you know that?"

"Um . . . no, sir," Nelle answered.

He nodded as if he was going back in time in his head. "Well, back then the roads were rough and it was really hard going. Often I had to ford a river and somehow keep the mail above water. Sometimes that meant holding the sack over my head, and that was on horseback."

He smiled at the memory and shook it off.

"One time, it was getting late and I was just trying to get home. The sun had set, but I could see somewhat by the light of the moon. I came to one of those enclosed wooden bridges, and the sound of my horse crossing those wooden planks was the only thing I could hear. I can still hear it."

He drove for a few more beats, then continued. "Anyway, I got to the other side and there was a Klansman, dressed head to toe in white, holding a torch and pointing a pistol straight at me. He ordered me off my horse."

Nelle looked at him, worried. "What'd you do?"

He shrugged. "I did as he said."

"Well, what happened?"

"He asked, 'Boy, you ever seen a man get hanged?'" A.C. rubbed his jaw. "Well, I hadn't, so I said, 'No, sir—but I am carrying the U.S. mail and I cannot stop for any reason, hanging or not.'

"The man had himself a good laugh, and then some more men came into view, also in white robes and hoods—except one. A colored boy, no older than me, dressed in rags, beaten and wild-eyed. His hands were tied and he was on the back of a pony.

"The man with the pistol said, 'Boys, this one says he's carrying the U.S. mail and can't be stopped! Don't that beat all?'

"They all laughed—except the colored boy, of course. His eyes were filled with terror and just pleading for help. 'I tell you what,' said the man. 'You're gonna stay and see justice served.'

"I stared at the scared boy. 'What's he done?' I asked.

"'That's not your concern,' said the man. 'This is Southern justice.'

"Well, I knew I couldn't get out of it, so I stood there and watched as they tied a rope up over a branch and around the boy's neck. I wanted to run so badly—I didn't want to see someone die for nothing. But the boy kept his eyes glued on me and I realized I had to stay, for him."

A.C. cleared his throat and struggled for words. "That boy . . .

begged for his life, but I was the only one who cared about him that night. There was nothing I could do. I knew I couldn't save him, but sometimes being a witness is just as important."

Nelle nodded as they drove up to what appeared to be an abandoned shack on the side of the road. A.C. stopped and pulled the brake. "I pray you'll never see the things I saw that night, Nelle. I quit the mail after that, and I may never do another capital case like this again. But sometimes, you just have to bear witness."

They walked hand in hand toward the shack as a woman Nelle assumed was Mrs. Ezell came out. When she saw the look on A.C.'s face, she broke down in tears.

30
Pecans on Ice

The hail finally stopped and Big Boy and Truman emerged from under the trees. Big Boy picked up a chunk of ice and put it in his mouth.

"What's it taste like?" asked Truman.

"Ice," he said after spitting it out. He looked around at the pecan trees they were hiding under. "Look where we are." He pointed at the darkened ramble of a house.

Truman looked. They were standing outside Sonny Boular's house. The same Sonny from the case they'd solved four years ago. The case that had put Sonny under house arrest for a year.

"Still creepy," said Truman. "You ever see him?"

"They say Sonny hasn't really been out of the house since . . . well, since his dad locked him away." He kicked a giant lump of hail and watched it crash into a tree. The impact knocked a few pecans into the dirt.

Big Boy looked at Truman. "As long as we're here . . ." he said.

"What? Pecans?"

"Sook wants some for her fruitcakes. We should take some," he said.

Truman loved Sook's fruitcakes, but that seemed so trivial at that moment.

"You know how she likes her pecans," said Big Boy, nudging him.

Truman sighed. "Fine. Let's get some pecans."

Almost nobody had seen the infamous Sonny for over four years, ever since Truman's going-away Halloween party. There were rumors that he snuck out and spied on people through their windows at night.

Truman stared at the gloomy house sitting ominously behind its bare trees. Bare except for the pecans.

"They don't even eat the pecans," said Big Boy.

"How d'you know?" asked Truman.

He kicked at the dirt. "I talk to him sometimes."

"Who, Sonny?"

He nodded. "He said we could take some pecans anytime we wanted. Well, anytime his father isn't around."

Truman looked at the house and sighed. "I don't know . . . what's the point of Christmas? Those fellas are gonna hang.

Nelle's feeling just awful. Jenny and them lost their home, and you all are put out because of it. Nina is going to come and get me sooner or later. We even lost that stupid Christmas tree. Maybe none of this would've happened if I hadn't've come back . . ."

Big Boy looked at him for the longest time. "Who *are* you?"

Truman was taken aback. "What?"

"Not what," said Big Boy. "Who."

Truman reached for Big Boy's glasses, cleaned them on his shirt, then put them back on his nose. "I'm Truman. Remember me?"

"I don't think so." He adjusted his glasses. "The Truman I knew wasn't a whiner."

Truman crossed his arms. He knew what Big Boy was trying to do. "I wouldn't call this whining. It's just the facts."

Big Boy shrugged. "Maybe. But here's what I know: you're the only one who can turn this all around."

Truman was confused. "What d'you mean?"

"I mean, ever since I've known you, you can turn the day upside down and make everyone smile. You can take a bad situation and spin it into a story that has everyone snorting milk through their noses."

Truman thought about it. Sook always said he had the gift for gab and could talk his way out of just about any situation. He knew he was a good storyteller and that he wanted to be a writer more than anything. "But what if I don't feel like telling *this* story?"

"That's not the point." Big Boy looked at him, incredulous. "Don't you know how much everyone missed you here? I ain't seen Sook smile in the two years since you left. And, well, I like Edison and all, but it just ain't the same. We can't even go to the picture show together 'cause they make him sit in the balcony. And Nelle, she's . . . you know."

"A girl."

"Yeah."

"Who has saved your butt more times than you can count," said Truman.

"Maybe."

Truman nodded. "Sook used to tell me I had to stop thinking just about myself. She always says that we only find happiness in the service of others."

"Do you believe that?" asked Big Boy.

Truman gazed at Sonny's house. "I don't know what I believe anymore. But right now, it sounds pretty good."

They walked up to the rickety overgrown fence that surrounded the property and stared at the lonesome home. "Looks empty," said Truman.

"Always does. Besides, I saw his ma and pa and sister at the town square." Big Boy slowly opened the gate and it squealed like a dying animal. He laughed. "Remember when you were so afraid to sneak in here that you ran all the way home?"

"I remember I ran because you screamed, that's what I remember," said Truman.

They scanned the yard and saw all the newly fallen pecans that had been knocked free by the hail. "What're we gonna carry them in? We don't have a bag," said Truman.

Big Boy was looking at the house. "I don't think that'll be a problem."

Truman heard a door close and spun around to see a cotton sack hanging from the front doorknob. Peeking through a small window in the door was a darkened face with eyes like a doll's.

"Maybe he heard you was here," said Big Boy.

Truman found himself drawn to the house. In all this time, he hadn't thought about Sonny; it was like he'd all but disappeared from his mind.

"You sure he's . . . okay?" asked Truman.

"Go see for yourself. He's harmless."

When he approached the porch, Truman could see a shadowy figure lurking behind the small window in the door. "You sure?" he asked.

"He's been waiting for you."

Truman stepped onto the front porch and paused to listen. When he didn't hear anything, he leaned forward to grab the sack.

The door handle clicked and the door cracked open as if the wind had pushed it in.

But there was no wind.

"Hello, Truman," said a voice so low he barely heard it.

Truman took a breath. "Hi, Sonny," he whispered back.

"I saw you," he said slowly. "When you came."

Truman looked at the front gate. "Well, the gate does need oiling . . ."

"No," said Sonny. "Before the fire. I knew you'd come back."

Truman could see Sonny's ghostly face back in the shadows. "You saw the fire?"

"Yes. I saw it start."

Truman leaned in closer and could barely make out Sonny's face in the dark. He seemed older and paler, his eyes sunken. But he was smiling.

"The fire? How'd it start?" Truman asked. "Did it come from Nelle's house?"

Sonny slowly shook his head. "A snake done it."

Truman took a step back. "A snake lit our house on fire?"

Sonny didn't answer.

"What'd it look like?" Truman asked.

"A real live wire," he said. "He flew away . . ."

Truman turned to Big Boy, who was listening.

"He flew away?" asked Big Boy.

"Like fireworks. Pow. *Pow* . . ."

"But—"

The door closed in Truman's face. "Sonny . . ." He knocked on the door. "Sonny?"

"He's off his rocker," said Big Boy. "He says strange things all the time. You know how he is."

Truman did. It was sad to see Sonny so cut off from the

world. "Come on. Let's get some pecans and get back to the farm."

"What about Nelle?"

Truman walked down the wooden steps and opened the bag. "We'll find her later. We'd best leave her be for now. I hope that judge lets those men see Christmas. It's the least he can do."

They gathered as many pecans as the bag would hold and set off on the long walk home.

31
Time's A-Wastin'

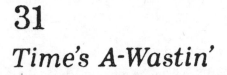

When Nelle woke up the next morning, her mother was in a panic. She was in the kitchen, creating quite a racket, tossing out pots and pans as their colored cook, Anna, followed her around in a frenzy.

"Where is he? Where is he?" her mother cried as she dug deeper into the pantry.

Nelle stood at the kitchen door, unsure what to do. "What're you looking for, Mama?"

"I can't find him! I simply cannot find him," she muttered.

Anna was beside herself. "She been saying this since she woke up. She won't tell me what she's looking for."

Nelle walked up to her mother and put her hand on her back. "Mama—"

Her mother pushed her away, almost knocking her over. "He's not here."

A.C. appeared in the doorway, disheveled from lack of sleep. "What on earth . . ."

He quickly assessed the situation, pulled his wife from the pantry, and turned her around to face him. He had run out of patience. "What are you looking for, Frances?"

Her eyes darted back and forth until he took her by the chin and steered her gaze to his. "Maybe I can help."

Her eyes focused on his and she caught her breath. "The Lord Baby Jesus. It's almost Christmas and he is nowhere to be found."

A.C. tilted his head. It took him a moment to realize she was looking for the nativity scene they put out every year. "My dear, he is where we always keep him."

He gently guided her through the kitchen into the hallway. He glanced at Nelle to see if she was all right. She nodded at him.

They walked over to the closet. Brother was watching from the end of the hall.

A.C. opened the closet and pulled out a box. Mother watched him anxiously as he rooted around and then drew out a small carved wooden Baby Jesus in his crib. "There, you see? Baby Jesus is quite all right."

She grabbed it from his hand and examined it closely. When she was satisfied, she held it to her chest. "There will be Christmas," she said.

A.C. smiled a painful smile.

Nelle wasn't so sure.

Sook was staring into the bag of pecans Truman had handed her. "You remembered! I was just fretting about fruitcakes and then you wake me up with these! I knew it was just a matter of finding the right time," she said.

"I'm just not sure it *is* the right time," said Truman morosely.

Sook went over and hugged him. "Well, you can't go hiding yourselves away like you did yesterday. We heard what happened. Jenny and Bud argued all night about it. Little Bit and Bama wouldn't talk to any of us. But we can only control what God puts in our hands. And what's in our hands right now are family and pecans."

"I guess," said Truman.

"Why, just yesterday, I was listening to Eleanor Roosevelt on the radio. Do you know what she said?" asked Sook.

Truman shrugged.

Sook scratched her head. "Hmm. Let me think . . . oh, I know! She said, 'Yesterday is history, tomorrow is a mystery, and today is a gift; that's why they call it the present!'"

"Did she really say that?" asked Tru.

"She did. So we must treat today like a gift and make the best of it. What do you say?"

Truman looked at Sook and remembered their discussion from the day before. *In service of others.* He decided he would try to change his attitude. "Okay, Sook. I'll try."

"Well, come on, then, we're already late," said Sook. "We won't have time to send one to Mrs. Roosevelt, but if we're lucky, we'll make enough to brighten the day for those who have too little to look forward to."

"I know a couple of people whose days could use some brightening," Tru said, thinking of the jailed father and son.

Sook knew who he was thinking about. "Amen to that."

They took over the kitchen, much to Bama's and Little Bit's consternation. "You can help or get out the way," Sook said as she poured the pecans onto the table.

They had no time for sorrow; there was work to do. "Oh, I'm helping," said Little Bit, knowing it bothered Bama. "Little Bit knows a thing or two about Miss Sook's fruitcakes, including her secret ingredient." She rooted about in the back of the pantry and pulled out a small bottle of Indian Joe's whiskey.

"Hush, don't tell anyone, least of all the children," said Sook.

Bama, not to be outdone, joined in too. "You gonna cook in my kitchen, you gon' need me to steer you right. Now, boy, smash them pecans into little bitty pieces," she said, pointing to Truman.

Sook was busy running around the kitchen, gathering her ingredients. Little Bit lit the stove and began humming to herself. Big Boy heard the ruckus, came in, and rolled up his sleeves, ready to work.

Jenny and Mary Ida poked their heads in. "What in the world is going on in here?" they asked.

"It's fruitcake time!" everyone sang in unison.

Jenny and Mary Ida looked at each other and smiled wistfully. At least one thing was right with the world. They joined in, helping to chop and stir and trying not to think of the past few days. Even Bud came around and watched calmly from the doorway.

Truman stood in the middle of it all and soaked it in. Maybe the curse had a silver lining after all.

32
Presents Galore

After hours of prepping and baking (eight cakes at a time in Mary Ida's giant stove), the first round of fruitcakes was done. While the next eight were placed in the oven, Truman, Sook, and Big Boy wrapped the first batch in butcher paper and string. The others napped, exhausted from all the goings-on.

At one point, Truman glanced up and saw Nelle standing at the back door. There was something peculiar about her.

"What happened to your hair?" Truman asked.

She ran her hand through her short bob. "I cut it off. I was tired of pretending to be someone else."

She was dressed in overalls and boots and a big winter jacket. Truman didn't say it, but she looked like a boy again.

Without missing a beat, Sook said, "Nelle Harper Lee, you best get in here. These cakes ain't gonna wrap themselves. Besides, one of 'em is for your family."

Truman scooted over on the bench and made space for her. Big Boy pushed an unwrapped cake to the empty spot.

"We need someone to help decorate these too," he said.

Queenie yipped at the screen door. Nelle came in, picked up the dog, and held him tight. She sat next to Tru and stared at the cake.

After a minute, she still hadn't begun. Truman leaned over and whispered in her ear, "I was thinking maybe we could take one over to the jailhouse and give it to the Ezells."

Nelle sucked in her breath. She placed Queenie back on the floor and started wrapping.

There was a pile of pictures Sook had cut out from old magazines—movie stars and scenes of country life. Sook sorted through them and came across an illustration of a house by a river at dusk. Through one of the windows she could see a family sitting down for supper. She handed it to Nelle. "This one reminds me of you. Maybe you can glue it to the wrapping," she said.

As the day grew long and all the cakes were wrapped and decorated, the spotlight switched to talk of presents and Christmas Day.

"It'll be funny having everyone over here for once," said Big Boy. "I don't believe we've ever had a bigger Christmas supper planned." He paused, looking at Sook and Bama. "You all do have it planned, right?"

"Well, while you all were running around dealing with killers on the loose," said Bama, "me and Lil' Bit were planning the big dinner. With Miss Sook, of course."

"What about you, Nelle?" asked Sook. "What do you think your daddy will make for supper?"

Nelle kept her eyes glued on her cake. "I don't think we'll be having much of a Christmas this year, Miss Sook. I've never seen A.C. so depressed. I think he can't even bring himself to think about a happy Christmas when two innocent men are headed for their end. On top of that, with all the excitement, Mama has been acting out, and A.C. says Christmas is making her a little out of sorts."

"So what're you saying? You gonna cancel Christmas?" asked Big Boy.

"I don't think the holidays are what's on his mind right now," she mumbled. "He hasn't even told anyone what he wants for Christmas yet."

"Well, what do you think he wants?" asked Truman.

She thought about it. "Shoot, I don't know. Right now, I'd give anything to see him smile again."

They all sat there quietly. Big Boy seemed upset. He pushed back his bench and walked out of the room.

"What's eating him?" Nelle asked.

Truman shrugged and admitted, "I haven't had time to think about presents either. We don't even have a tree yet."

Nelle shook her head. "After what happened last time, I wouldn't recommend going to get one."

Sook smiled. "House isn't complete till you got a tree by the fireplace and presents underneath it. I wouldn't worry about it. A tree will be here soon."

Truman looked at her. "What do you mean, a tree will be here soon?"

Sook smiled slyly. "You'll see."

Just then, Big Boy came and sat back down. He slapped his hand on the table. "It's settled."

"What's settled?" asked Truman.

He turned to Nelle. "I asked my ma and pa and they said it's all fine, the more the merrier."

"What does that mean?" asked Nelle.

"It means you and your family are gonna have Christmas with us," said Big Boy. "We already got a full house, and a few more won't matter in the end. We won't take no for an answer!"

Nelle knew Big Boy could be stubborn once an idea popped into that thick skull of his. She nodded. "Okay, then."

Big Boy had been expecting a fight. "I mean it, Nelle. You're coming over for Christmas supper if I gotta ride you over on them two mules—"

"Big Boy!" she said.

"What?" he said back.

They stared at each other till she smiled. "Does that mean I'm back in the boys' club?"

Big Boy blinked, looked at Truman, then back at Nelle. "You never left."

• • •

When Nelle walked out of the farmhouse, she felt lighter. She knew that when the burden of Christmas was off A.C.'s shoulders, he would feel lighter too. And Mother tended to behave better outside the home, especially if there was a good piano. Mary Ida had a swell one that she'd inherited from her grandmother.

Nelle's mood was buoyed when she saw that the winter clouds had broken and the sun was actually peeking through the gray. It shined brightly on her as she headed home. She'd forgotten what her shadow looked like in all the gloom of the past weeks. Even though it was still cold as heck, the sun warmed her face, and she could hear the occasional icicle fall from a nearby tree and crash to the ground.

She heard another sound: the sound of digging. As she headed across the field, she spotted Edison, elbow-deep in the ground, digging his hole.

"Edison, what in the world are you doing?" she asked. "You know you cain't dig a hole to China. That'd take you weeks!"

"Ain't digging no hole to Ch-China, Miss Nelle," he answered.

"Well, where you digging to, then?" she asked.

Edison stopped and wiped his brow. "Not wh-where, what."

"What?"

He showed off his hole. It was about four feet wide. Beyond that, there were four sticks planted in the ground ten feet around him. "Gonna build me a p-pool."

"A pool? What kinda fool idea is that? It's too cold to swim!"

"Seeing what h-happened to the Ezells got m-me thinking. There's no time to w-waste. It c-could all go away, like th-that!" He snapped. "They won't let us in their p-pool? Well, fine. I'll make m-my own, then. And you're w-welcome to s-swim in it. Prob'ly take me till s-summer ta f-finish. Then they c-can reopen the town p-pool for the likes of B-Boss and them."

Nelle watched as Edison stubbornly started to dig in the frozen ground again. "Need help?" she asked.

"No, Miss Nelle. Not enough r-room for two yet. But when it gets b-big enough, you can c-come help."

"All right, then. See you when I see you." She was about to head off when she heard something rustling through the brush at the edge of the forest. She stopped to listen, thinking it might be a bobcat or even a bear.

When she saw something big and brown wedging its way backward through the dense growth, she jumped into the hole with Edison and pulled him down out of sight. He was about to say something, but she held her finger to her lips. "Shh . . ."

They both peeked over the lip of the hole and watched as the great beast struggled to pull something out into the open. Maybe a bear had caught a deer and was trying to drag it into the field to feast on.

Suddenly, with a yank, the beast fell back into the dirt. It was wearing a big brown overcoat and a fuzzy brown wool cap and was dragging a big ol' Christmas tree by its trunk.

It was worse than a bear. It was Boss.

33
Tree Delivery

Truman nearly fell over when he saw Boss dragging that tree toward the farmhouse. Boss still wore a large bandage on his head but otherwise seemed fine. Even though the tree was a good eight feet tall, he dragged it across the icy dirt like it was a large rag doll.

Truman knew instantly that it was his tree.

When Boss came close enough, he happened to look up and see Truman watching him through the front window. No emotions crossed his large flat face. He just dropped the tree and stood there.

"A right friendly boy, that one," said Sook, looking over Truman's shoulder. She reached into her sweater pocket and pulled out twenty-five cents. "Now go pay him."

"You asked Boss to fetch us that tree?" he asked suspiciously.

"Hm, I don't think so . . ." said Sook thoughtfully. "Perhaps his mother asked him to do it. She is a prideful woman. Even though they're poor, they need to show they can contribute. Now go pay him," she repeated. She put the coins into his hand and closed it.

She was a sly one. "If he's so prideful, won't paying him be an insult?" asked Truman.

"Nonsense. A man needs to get paid for his labor. Otherwise, it's like a form of servitude," she answered.

She pushed him out the front door and closed it behind him. Truman turned back with a look that pleaded for mercy, but Sook just smiled through the window and motioned him on.

He took a breath and exhaled. Then marched toward certain doom.

Boss watched him without expression.

The closer Truman went, the bigger Boss grew, until he towered over him like a giant oak tree. Truman stood in his shadow but didn't quite know what to say.

"That the same tree?" Truman blurted out.

Boss glared even harder. "What do you think?"

He thought yes. Boss would give him the tree to show he was the bigger man, even though it should have been obvious.

Truman held out his hand with the coins in it. "Sook wants you to have this. For dragging that thing all the way over."

Boss glanced down at the shiny coins in Truman's hand.

Truman's arm was growing tired from holding his arm out. But Boss didn't take the money.

"You an' me ain't done," Boss said, slow and surly.

Then he turned and walked back the way he'd come.

Truman tried to swallow but his throat went dry. "It wasn't *my* idea," he said.

He watched Boss get smaller and smaller until he disappeared into a thicket of trees. Big Boy was suddenly right behind Truman.

"What'd he say?" said Big Boy.

Truman decided not to tell him that this Christmas might be his last. "Merry Christmas."

Big Boy laughed and went over to inspect the tree. "Go figure. Well, at least you got your tree back. Things might be looking up after all."

Truman gazed at the tree and remembered how perfect it had seemed a couple of days ago. Now it just felt sad, though it was no worse for wear than before.

"Oh my! Looks like Santa paid an early visit," said Sook from the porch. She ambled out into the wintry air, wrapped in a quilt, to inspect the tree. She was impressed. "Twice as tall as a boy, so they can't fiddle with the star. Full and plump like a Christmas hog. Let's get it inside and see what we can do with it."

Big Boy and Truman grabbed the base and Sook took hold of the top. Even Queenie came out to tug on a branch.

"Oh my, what a lovely tree!" said Mary Ida when she came upon them pulling it through the front door.

Jenny was sitting in the parlor, looking wistful, as if thinking of all the things she'd lost. But when she heard the commotion and wandered into the living room, a smile crept across her face.

The boys had propped the tree up nice and tall in the corner by the wood stove. They'd left a trail of needles and dirt across the floor, but no one seemed to mind. The smell of pine in the house changed everything.

It was Christmas Eve, and the tree was up and decorated with strings of popcorn, paper angels, candles, and a star woven from straw. Edison and his father had come around to see it; Edison couldn't stop marveling at the wonder of it all.

"Boss g-gave it over to y-you? Just like *th-that?*" He shook his head. "D-do that mean I g-got to invite him into my p-pool?" Nobody knew quite what he was going on about, but everyone seemed delighted by the tree, except Tru.

"Tru, dear, don't fret. You still worried about Boss? Or them Ezell men?" asked Sook.

Truman wasn't sure. "It just feels strange to have Christmas this year."

"I know what you mean, Truman." Jenny sighed. "People haven't had that same Christmas cheer. They've been out of work and haven't been spending money in my store, that's for sure.

And now that the house is gone . . . and Callie too . . ." She couldn't finish her thought.

"I don't know what's going to happen to me. I just know I don't want to go back to that school," said Truman.

"Oh, hush. You gonna stay here, Tru," said Sook. "That's what I've decided. It's my Christmas present to you."

Truman loved hearing Sook say that, but deep down, he couldn't let himself believe such a thing.

"Quiet, Sook. Don't be making promises you can't keep," said Jenny.

"Well, why not?" said Sook. "Our Trueheart has a right to be happy. Certainly his parents don't give two hoots about him."

"You don't know that," said Jenny. "Lillie Mae may be many things, but she's still his mother, and it's not for us to say, even if we'd like to." She gestured toward Truman. "If the Lord intends him to stay, well, I wouldn't say no. Could use another man around here."

Just then, Bud came out in his red long johns and a Santa hat. With his big white beard and broad belly, he looked like Santa, all right, but a lazy one who liked to plop down in a chair and gaze into the fire. "What're you all gabbing about?"

Jenny shook her head. "Honestly, Bud. It's one thing to dress like that at home. To do so at someone else's house is uncouth."

"That's all right," said Jennings Sr. as he lit his pipe. "You all are family. And we've seen worse than Bud's long johns."

Even in the kitchen, a kindly mood took over Bama and

Little Bit, a feeling of a Christmas truce and perhaps hope that they'd erased Truman's curse. They talked in hushed tones about the next day's feast, but both had heard about the Ezells, which took the wind out of their sails. Still, they perked up a little when Bud started playing Christmas carols on the piano.

All things considered, it wasn't a bad way to spend Christmas Eve.

34
Christmas Morning

Truman woke with a start. Something felt different; there was a quiet to the air. Big Boy snored gently with his face smashed up against the wall. Queenie nestled between them like a warm bundle, keeping their feet toasty.

Truman slid out of the bed, careful not to let the squeak of the springs wake his cousin. The wood floors were frozen to the touch, even through his wool socks. He padded out into the main room, where he could still smell the scent of pine and firewood.

There was the tree and, under it, presents. Lots of presents. Some wrapped in fancy paper, others in decorated newsprint. *Where did those come from?* he thought.

But there was something else. He walked over to the front door and placed his hand against the door frame. A chill leaked gently through the cracks. He put his hand on the knob and turned.

When the door blew open, puffs of white snow danced about him like fireflies, settling on the floor. Truman took a step out onto the porch and held his breath.

It had snowed all night. The dirty slush was gone. In its stead was white, as far as the eye could see. Not a footstep or a sound except the gentle padding of snowflakes as they hit the earth.

It was a white Christmas after all.

The sun was just creeping up in the east, though you wouldn't know it by the quiet gray that covered it. Truman walked out to the edge of the porch and felt the chill on his toes. He stepped off and watched his feet disappear into the white powder. It felt like walking on clouds.

Tru stared up into the sky and opened his mouth as wide as it could go. He could feel the snowflakes settle on his face and melt on his tongue. They tasted like winter.

He didn't care that he was dressed in a nightshirt. He let himself fall backward into the snow, sending up a puff of fine powder all around him. He'd always wanted to make a snow angel, so that was just what he did. He could feel the snow trickling down his neck, but it didn't matter.

There was the sound of little feet, and the next thing he knew, Queenie pounced on him and disappeared into a snowbank. The dog's head popped up, decked out in a hat of white and a snow beard, to boot. He barked, bounded back onto Truman, and licked his face.

"Good gosh almighty, can you believe it!"

Truman tilted his head up and saw Sook on the front porch.

"The Lord granted me my wish. A white Christmas! I have lived on this earth for sixty years and never once have I seen such a thing!" she said.

She leaped off the porch and danced around in her tennis shoes, sending up a flurry of white. Soon, Big Boy, awakened by the noise, found himself diving in, making snowballs, and firing them off at Tru and Sook, who eagerly returned fire. The snow was far too fine for a good snowball fight, so it was more like playing war with powdered sugar.

After all their running about, they noticed their teeth beginning to chatter (all except Sook, who'd left her teeth in a glass by the bed), so they went in and gathered around the fireplace to warm up. The smell of chicory coffee floated through the air as Bama and Little Bit busied themselves in the kitchen. Jenny and Mary Ida emerged, took one look at the wet, smiling faces, and asked what on earth they had been doing, to which Tru and Big Boy pointed out the window and answered, *"Snow!"*

The women were both staring out the window in wonderment when Bud and Jennings Sr. wandered out, dressed to the nines in their Sunday best.

"Well, well, looks like Santa found us after all. Even brought us a little snow. We opening presents or what?" said Bud.

Truman's eyes lit up. "Can we?"

"After church," said Mary Ida. "We cannot exchange gifts until we leave a gift for Baby Jesus at the manger."

Truman knew that was the rule, but rules were made for bending. "What if we each opened one?" he asked innocently.

"Now, why would we do that?" asked Mary Ida.

"It's a tradition. In some countries, I mean," he said, matter-of-fact. "Or so I read."

"Sounds like one of your fanciful stories, if you ask me," she said, grinning.

Sook held up her hand. "No, Trueheart, we mustn't. There are folks out there in need, and we must tend to them first before we celebrate our own good fortune."

Truman just looked at Sook. "But you've lost everything too. And I—"

"—have a roof over your head, food for your belly, and family who cares for you," said Jenny proudly. "Sook is right. We shall spread some goodwill to those in need."

"With what?" asked Big Boy.

"Fruitcake, of course!" said Sook with her toothless grin. "Ain't never been a fruitcake that couldn't brighten someone's day."

35
Fruitcake for All

Before coming to Big Boy's farm, Sook had stopped leaving her house. She had grown afraid of the outside world. But once the house was gone, Sook had nothing to cling to except her people.

Before the house had burned, she'd almost never been in a car, but here she was, sitting in the front seat of Jenny's car for the third time that week, happy as could be. Jenny drove down the snow-covered road with Mary Ida, Truman, Big Boy, and all the fruitcakes they could fit. The idea was they'd go to church and hand out fruitcakes to everyone on Sook's list, which included the neighbors, the mayor, the preacher, and the under-taker, with whom she wanted to keep on good terms for when her time came. Other cakes would be saved for later and given to Boss for his family and some of the poor souls in Mudtown.

Truman hadn't been to church in a long time, since neither Nina nor Joe went, but he did enjoy the spectacle of it all: the town choir singing "O Come, All Ye Faithful," the decorations, and, of course, the giant nativity scene, for which some of Monroeville's finest dressed up to play Mary, Joseph, and the three wise men. Real farm animals were brought in: a cow, a sheep, a pig, and, instead of a camel, a llama from Mobile with a hump added for effect. Baby Jesus was played by a lightbulb placed deep in a crib of straw, because the year before, when a real baby had been used, it had spit up all over Mary's gown, which spooked the pig, which scared the cow, which sent all the animals scurrying into the crowd.

Fruitcakes were handed out to many as they came in. But one party was missing: Nelle and her family.

After the sermon, as everyone mingled out front and talked about rebuilding and the wonders of snow, Truman couldn't help but gaze in the direction of Nelle's house.

"Where do you suppose she is?" said Truman.

Big Boy shrugged. "Search me. Maybe we should check on—"

Before he could finish, Truman began to walk down the road, listening to his shoes squeak on the virgin snow. Big Boy, who was holding two cakes, turned to his pa, who was watching Truman wander off. Jennings Sr. nodded as if he understood.

"Go on, then. I figure we'll be here awhile," he said to Big Boy.

Big Boy followed but stayed back a few paces. When Truman turned the corner, Big Boy turned the corner. He trailed Tru down Alabama Avenue until he could see the remains of Jenny's house.

Nothing had changed since the night it had all burned down, except that the charred ruins were now covered with a fine layer of white. It looked like a cake of sorts. Beyond it were the remains of the double chinaberry tree, now just a couple of blackened stumps.

The only thing left intact was the horse-bone wall that divided their properties.

When Big Boy caught up to Tru, he realized Tru was looking not at the ruins but at what was beyond them: Nelle's shed. And coming from the shed was a *clickity-clack* sound he hadn't heard for a long while: a typewriter.

They walked quietly up to the shed and peered through the window. There sat Nelle, bundled up in a lumberjack coat and wool cap, typing away with two fingers.

"Nelle?" said Truman, tapping on the glass.

Nelle stopped typing and looked up.

"It's good to see you writing again," said Truman.

"Writing don't come easy to me, Tru. Not like you."

"I don't believe that, Nelle. You're the best storyteller I know," he said earnestly.

"This is different," she said, and started typing again.

The boys pressed their faces to the window. "Why're you sitting out here instead of inside with your family?" asked Big Boy.

She continued clacking away. "I'm writing a letter to the governor, if you must know."

"Like a Christmas card?" asked Big Boy.

She didn't answer.

"Where is everyone? And how come you weren't in church?" asked Truman.

She paused to read a sentence. "A.C.'s in jail. And Brother and them have taken Mama down to Pensacola, on account of— well, just because."

Truman's jaw dropped. "A.C.'s in jail? What for?"

"He's there to make sure the Ezells make it through Christmas all right."

Truman couldn't make sense of her. "All right? But they're in jail."

"Well, there's some who'd like to do 'em harm right now. That's why I'm writing to the governor. Get them a, whatchamacallit —a *reprieve*."

"But who would want to do 'em harm now? It's Christmas, fer cryin' out loud," said Big Boy.

Nelle took a good long look at the boys. "You know as well as me who would. Why, one of 'em is eating at your table today, which, considering everything, don't seem much like Christmas to me."

"Boss? Why don't his kin leave well enough alone? Ain't the Ezells suffered enough?" said Big Boy.

Nelle shrugged.

"So what's A.C. doing?" asked Truman.

"He's holding down the fort because everyone else down at the jail took Christmas morning off!" said Nelle.

Truman threw up his hands. "Well, what're we doing here, then?" he asked.

Nelle knew Truman was right. What *was* she doing here? She typed one more sentence, pulled the sheet of paper out of the typewriter, and blew on it.

She emerged from the shed. "Right—let's go," she said, folding the letter in two.

"Wait," said Truman.

"Wait? Didn't you want to go down to the jail?" asked Big Boy.

Truman's mind started to race. If there was one thing he had a talent for, it was getting out of a jam. Whenever a cockamamie idea popped into his head, his blue eyes seemed to glow two shades brighter.

"I have an idea," he said. "Meet me in front of the jail." He ran back toward the church.

"Where you going?" shouted Big Boy.

"You'll see!" said Truman.

Nelle and Big Boy hadn't seen him this excited since he'd come home. "What d'ya think he's aiming to do?" asked Big Boy.

Nelle shrugged. "Don't know. But it better be good."

She suddenly noticed that Big Boy was holding two fruit-cakes. "Are those what I think they are?"

Big Boy nodded.

"Come on, then. I ain't much for fruitcake, but I know some who might be," said Nelle.

And with that, they headed off to jail.

36
Christmas in Jail

Nelle had been in the jailhouse many times before, always with A.C. at her side. Monroeville had one sheriff and one deputy, and that was the entire police force. There wasn't much need for more than that. Not a lot happened here, except for an occasional drunk overstaying his welcome.

The jailhouse door was locked and the front office appeared to be empty. Nelle and Big Boy peered through the window but couldn't see anyone inside.

"Are you sure he's here?" asked Big Boy. "Maybe they moved someplace else."

"They're here. Let's go around back," said Nelle.

Big Boy followed Nelle around the side of the building,

holding on to his cakes. When they came to a plain window high up on the wall with bars in it, she stopped.

"Give me a boost," she said.

Big Boy's hands were full, but he put his cakes down on the snow, walked over to the wall, and bent over. "Don't mess up my Sunday best," he said.

His Sunday best was his same old clothes but with a tie. Nelle took off one shoe, stepped on his knee, then got a leg up onto his back and stood up on his shoulders. Big Boy struggled to stay upright.

"Come on, now, stand up straight," she said.

"You sure are heavy for a girl," he said, standing as straight as he could.

Nelle reached as high as her arms would go, but she was still a foot short. "Can you jump?" she asked.

"No, I can't jump! You jump."

She scowled but bent down and leaped. Had she missed the ledge, she would have come crashing down on Big Boy. But her left hand caught hold and she pulled herself up till she could peek over the ledge.

When her eyes adjusted to the dark inside, she saw A.C. sitting in a cell with Frank and Brown Ezell, all of them staring up at her.

A.C. did not look happy.

Nelle dropped to the ground and put her shoe on; then she and Big Boy rushed around to the back door, where no one would see them. They waited until they heard footsteps, followed by the sound of locks being undone. When the door cracked open, A.C. peered out beyond them to see if anyone was watching. When he saw that the coast was clear, he grabbed them and pulled them inside.

"I told you not to come!" he said sternly. "Why are you here? Why are you not at Big Boy's?"

"I'm sorry, A.C. I was gonna go, but I decided to write a letter instead, and then Big Boy and Tru came to fetch me and, well, they said we should come here 'cause, well, nobody should be alone on Christmas, not them and not you."

A.C. grimaced but wasn't angry. He checked the alley once again and locked the door behind them.

"What's this about a letter?" he said.

"A letter to the governor. To ask for a reprieve," she said, handing it over. "I wrote it."

He unfolded it to take a look. They were standing in a bare room that held a single cell made of iron bars, a desk, and a few chairs. Nelle saw the Ezell men watching her, then realized they were not alone. Mrs. Ezell sat behind them in the shadows.

"Hello, missus," said Nelle.

Big Boy stepped forward. "We brought you some fruitcakes. We made 'em ourselves. Figured you'd be hungry."

He walked toward the open cell door but didn't want to step in. Big Boy extended his arms and held the cakes out for Brown, who was closest. He looked hollow and forlorn, but he reached up and took them.

Big Boy stepped back quickly. Brown sniffed at the cakes,

unsure what they were. "It's okay, they're good," said Big Boy. "I tasted them myself."

"Hand me one," said Brown's father, Frank, his voice almost gone. Brown handed one over and Frank scooted next to his wife and sat beside her. Her face was puffy, probably from crying. They unwrapped the parcel. Frank offered it to his wife, who broke off a small piece and nibbled on it. She nodded and smiled.

"You're right. Sure is good," she said. "Thank you."

Big Boy beamed. "I made that one myself, I think."

Frank tried some as well and nodded in approval. "Got a little kick to it. Bet you been over to Indian Joe's, ain't ya?"

"You know him?" asked Big Boy.

"We been by there once or twice. You get to meet everyone along the river sooner or later." He chuckled. "Never know what you'll find in these waterways . . ."

He stopped chewing and grew solemn.

Brown stared at the cake he held in his hand. "Can't eat this. Just reminds me of all the Christmases I'll never get to." He put it on the bench next to him. "That's cruel, to make a man think of that."

Big Boy and Nelle were taken aback.

"Hush, child," said his mama. "They only meant well. Just like Mr. A.C."

"Yeah, but meaning well ain't gonna keep us alive, is it?" said Brown, gazing at the floor. "Meaning well don't mean nothing unless it gets us free."

A.C. finished reading Nelle's letter. "He's right. This is well intentioned, Nelle. But I don't think it will do any good. The governor is unlikely to reprieve a couple of Negroes found guilty of murder, especially in an election year."

"I was just trying to help," she said softly.

Frank stood up. "I know you were, Miss Nelle. And that do mean something, even if Brown here don't think so. When you don't have much time left, it's the little things that make what you got all the better," he said. "May I see that letter?"

A.C. handed it to him. Frank unfolded it and stared at it until A.C. realized he couldn't read.

"I can read it to you if you like—" said A.C.

"No, no. I can feel what it says," Frank said. After Frank stared at it for a few moments, Brown stood up and took the letter from him.

"Let me see that," he said. He sat back down and read it.

"'Dear Governor Miller,'" he read aloud. "'My name is Nelle Harper Lee and I am twelve years old. I am writing on account of it is my fault that these two men' . . ." He looked at Nelle and grimaced, then continued reading. "'Frank Ezell and Brown Ezell were found guilty of killing Mr. Northrup. It is my fault because they didn't do it and it is only 'cause I opened my big fat mouth' . . ."

He closed letter and gritted his teeth. "Come here, miss."

Nelle turned to her father, who nodded. She walked over and paused in the cell door.

Brown looked her in the eye. "There's plenty of people whose fault it is for us being here. My own, in particular, for wanting to stop at that market to get a knickknack for Mama and some licorice, because I had a hankerin'. Didn't need it, shouldn't be spending my money on it. Wanted it, is all. If I wasn't so—"

"Son," his father interrupted. "Wanting licorice ain't no crime."

He nodded. "Nope, wanting licorice ain't no crime. Neither is a jury made up of twelve white men, including the victim's son." He laughed bitterly. "Now, don't that beat all?"

"I'm sorry," said Nelle.

"It ain't your fault, Miss Nelle, any more than it is mine," Brown said. "We just in the wrong place, wrong time, is all."

There was a long awkward pause. Nelle didn't know what to say. *Merry Christmas* wasn't gonna cut it. She reached into her front pocket, pulled something out, and handed it to Brown.

It was the Santa figurine from the river shore. He held it in his palm as if someone had handed him a chunk of gold. He shook his head and laughed. "Don't that beat all . . ." he said again. He walked over to his mama and gave it to her. "That's for you," he said softly.

She clutched it to her chest.

Nelle stepped away and walked back to A.C. He put his hand on her shoulder and watched the Ezells talk in hushed tones to one another.

"Word," A.C. whispered in Nelle's ear. "*P* and five."

She thought about it, then muttered, *"Proud."*

He squeezed her hand, then led her over to Big Boy. A.C. whispered to both of them, "Now I think it's time you two to get back to the farm. You have your people waiting for you, Big Boy. And despite all this, life goes on. You have to live it the best way you know how."

"But what about you?" asked Nelle. "We can't leave you here."

Her father rubbed her hair and just seemed to notice it was short again. But he didn't say anything about it. "I've seen plenty of Christmases in my time, eaten too many turkeys and hams to remember. I'll see many more, God willing. If I miss this one, so be it. You'll just have to have it without me."

Nelle crossed her arms and stamped her foot. She was not going to budge. "No, sir. You said sometimes you just gotta bear witness. Well, today I'm the bear."

A.C. had seen that look before. It was more stubborn than Big Boy's mules. He'd tried many times to defeat that bear; he always lost.

He stood up tall, took out his pocket watch, and checked the time. "You might get hungry."

"I don't care," she said.

He tapped the watch in his palm. "I know there's a present or two waiting for you over there. I conferred with Santa myself . . ."

"Phooey—what do you think I am, six? There ain't no such thing as Santa and you know it. Presents can wait."

A look came over his face. It was a look she rarely saw but she surely recognized. It was a look of gratitude.

"And you, Big Boy? You've no dog in this fight. Go home and be with your family." He turned to the Ezells. "In the end, family is all that matters."

Big Boy was torn. He wanted to go home, but he felt bad for leaving.

Everyone flinched when someone started pounding on the front door. "Open up! Open up in there!" said a deep voice.

Frank and Brown stood up, unsure of what to do. A.C. walked over and calmly locked the cell door with Mrs. Ezell inside. "Sorry, just being safe." He pocketed the key and looked at Nelle and Big Boy. "Stay here. If there's trouble, go out the back door. Go to the church and get help."

When A.C. moved toward the front room, Nelle and Big Boy ignored his command and followed.

He reached the front door, and the banging continued. "Open up!" But this time, the voice was high-pitched and odd. A.C. peered out the peephole.

On the other side was Truman. "For crying out loud—" said A.C. He unlocked the door and stared at Truman's smiling face. He was holding a fruitcake.

"Truman! What are you doing here?" said A.C. "You gave us all quite a fright. Do you have any idea—"

Only when he glanced to his left did he see Truman was not alone. Standing to the side were Jenny, Mary Ida, Bud, and Sook, who was holding Queenie.

"Oh. Hello. What, um, are you all doing here on Christmas morning?" said A.C.

Sook went up to him. "Well, it's like this, Mr. Amasa. Preacher reminded us what the spirit of Christmas is all about.

Family, yes. Being good to your neighbors, uh-huh. Being kind to those in need—now, that's the true spirit of Christmas!"

Jenny stepped forward. "We have been the beneficiaries of that kindness ourselves after our house burned down and now we feel, thanks to Truman, that we should extend that kindness to others."

A.C. was taken aback. "Well, that's very noble of you, Miss Jenny, Sook. But I don't know what you can do here . . ."

Jenny placed her hand on his arm. "Sometimes it's not knowing what to do, but just being there. So Mary Ida and I have instructed Jennings Sr. to bring Christmas here."

Nelle smiled at Truman. "Was that your idea?"

He shrugged. "It just seemed like the right thing to do, that's all."

Big Boy nodded. "Well, I think it's a fine idea. Are they really bringing everything here?"

And before he could answer, Jennings Sr. pulled up in his pickup, with Bama and Little Bit squeezed together in front. In the back sat Edison and Cousin with all the food everyone had spent the morning cooking. Tied in the back of the flatbed lay the Christmas tree.

For once A.C. was speechless. He squeezed Jenny's hand and patted Truman on the head. "I've seen many things in my day, but this is a new one. Christmas in jail." He grew serious. "You realize it's not exactly safe here. No telling who's gonna come for them."

Jenny stood tall. "Nobody is going to come here on Christmas Day and bother that family. And if they do, they'll have to go through me."

"And me," said Mary Ida.

"And me," said Truman.

A.C. nodded as everyone chimed in. "I have no doubt," he said.

When Mr. and Mrs. Ezell and their son saw the families enter the room, they were befuddled. When they saw the feast they carried in with them, they were shocked. Bud and Jennings Sr. brought in the giant ham, a rare treat these days. Bama and Little Bit brought in butter beans, crowders, and okra. Truman had the corn bread and gravy, Jenny and Mary Ida, the candied yams and sweet tea. Sook carried in her specialty: the stuffing. When Edison and his dad and A.C. brought in the decorated tree, it was almost too much.

They pushed together some desks and made a table, covered it with Mary Ida's finest linens and some candles. The Ezells came out of the cell as everyone gathered around and held hands. This was not a merry occasion, but it felt more meaningful than any Christmas Truman or Nelle or Big Boy had ever had.

A.C. said the Lord's Prayer, then looked Frank and Brown in the eye and said, "This is not over. I plan to appeal this decision to a higher court. I will not let this go, you'll see." The Ezells nodded but were not exactly hopeful. They knew how things worked in the South.

Jenny started singing "Silent Night" and everyone joined in. Even Brown, for the moment, let go of his anger and decided, for his mother's sake, to enjoy one last Christmas.

As they sat around stuffing their faces, Truman scanned the room. It was not the Christmas he'd expected. But it felt real. It wasn't about stockings and mangers, but about people. About reaching out. About bearing witness.

He sat there admiring the scene, and his eyes fell on the tree propped in the corner, decorations and all. "I guess Boss wouldn't dare show up here," he said.

Sook dropped a spoonful of butter beans. "Heavens to Betsy! We forgot about Boss!"

"What do you mean?" asked Truman.

"Nobody told him we switched Christmas," she said. "He's probably back at the farmhouse, sitting there all alone wondering where we are."

Truman knew the next thing that would come out of her mouth.

"Well, we're just gonna have to go get him, then," she said.

37
Boss Time

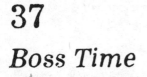

"You think he'll really be there?" Truman asked. For backup, Nelle and Big Boy had piled into Jennings Sr.'s truck with him and Bud as they headed to the farm.

"Well, Little Chappie, I hope so," said Bud. "Sook might never shut up about it if we don't find him."

As they parked in front of the farmhouse, Nelle spotted a set of footprints crossing the virgin snow. "Somebody came out of the forest there."

Big Boy climbed out and saw how big the footprints were. "Could be the Abominable Snowman, for all we know."

The footsteps led up to the front door. "What if he's mad?" asked Nelle.

"Why'd he be mad?" asked Bud.

"Wouldn't you be if somebody invited you to Christmas dinner and there was none? Maybe he thinks we played a big joke on him to embarrass him."

"I'd say you're letting your imagination get the best of you," said Bud. "He'll understand."

Truman knew making Boss look like a fool was never a good idea. Still, it was four against one, even if Boss outweighed the four.

They walked into the front room. Where the tree had been, all that was left was a small pile of presents, which they were planning to open later. However, it looked like someone had beaten them to it.

"He opened the presents!" cried Truman.

The items had clearly been gone through. "Don't jump to any conclusions," said Bud.

They heard a noise from the kitchen.

Bud walked down the hallway and the others followed. They all thought some variation of the same thing: *Boss wouldn't beat up an old man, would he?*

Then they heard something they didn't expect.

Singing.

At first they thought maybe it was Jenny's Victrola phonograph player, but that had been destroyed in the fire. Someone was singing "O Come, All Ye Faithful" in an angelic high-pitched voice that took everyone's breath away.

Bud slowly pushed open the kitchen door, and none of them

could quite believe what they were seeing: Boss Henderson, dressed in a ratty brown suit a couple of sizes too small for his enormous frame, his hair combed like wild brush mushed to the side, was seated at the kitchen table, eyes closed, singing. On the table was a mishmash of leftover food that he'd apparently scrounged up, the Christmas kite that Sook had made for Truman, and a glass paperweight that was one of the only possessions Jenny had saved from the fire.

They stood there frozen in disbelief till he finished his song, sweet as can be. Then he released an enormous belch that broke the spell.

After a good, long awkward pause, Bud quietly closed the door and counted to five, then turned and cupped his hand and called in the opposite direction, "Hello? Anybody home?" He started clomping his feet on the wooden floor, quietly at first, then louder.

From inside the kitchen they heard a scramble, followed by the back door opening and shutting. Bud reopened the door and saw the empty chair and the food. Jenny's glass paperweight was gone. All that remained was Truman's kite.

No one knew what to make of it until the there was a knock at the front door. "Hello?" said a low, gruff voice.

Boss.

Bud headed back to the front room. The others followed.

"Hello, you must be" — Bud swung open the door and found himself looking into Boss's chest — "Peter?"

Boss cleared his throat, embarrassed by the whole situation. Truman could tell he'd never worn a suit before. It actually looked painfully tight and uncomfortable.

"Yeah," he said. Then a moment later, "Yes, sir."

His jaw tightened up when he saw the others.

"I'm sorry we weren't here earlier," said Bud. "Did you wait for us long?" As soon as he said it, he knew he hadn't given his guest an out. "I mean to say, our plans changed unexpectedly and we decided to have Christmas elsewhere and realized nobody had told you."

Boss seemed confused. "No, I just came, um, right now. So . . . you ain't having Christmas?"

"Not exactly," said Truman. "We're having Christmas, all right, just not here."

"We're having it at the jail," Nelle spat out nervously. "'Cause that's where A.C. is."

Boss's eyes shifted and a series of emotions flashed across his face. "Why would you—" He paused, his mind racing. "Um, you shouldn't do that," he finally said.

Bud tilted his head. "Now, why is that, Peter?" he asked.

Boss looked at the floor. "'Cause that where them ni—" He caught himself. "You just don't wanna be down there, is all."

"Why?" said Nelle. "'Cause your daddy and his friends are going down there to cause trouble? Don't you know them folks have suffered enough? Cain't you just leave 'em be?"

Boss didn't answer.

Truman noticed Jenny's glass paperweight in Boss's hand. "And where'd you get *that*?"

Boss looked in his hand and realized he'd been found out. He gave the paperweight to Bud. "I was just—looking at it." His face was red. "You shouldn't make people look like dummies by inviting them to things you don't intend to be there for."

Bud held up his hands. "Now, now, we're all friends here."

"He ain't my friend," said Nelle.

Boss's face grew tight. "Least I don't go round knocking people out, you little—"

He didn't say it, mostly because Truman stepped up to him and Nelle and Big Boy followed, even if they didn't know why.

Boss looked down at Truman and his friends. "Look," Truman said nervously. "You can clearly beat us all to a pulp. We weren't trying to make you look bad or anything. Sook really wanted you to come over. She said people only hate each other 'cause they don't know any better. Because they don't know each other."

He gulped, looked over to Nelle for reassurance. She nodded. "I mean, look at us," said Truman. "Who woulda thought me and her would be friends? Nobody. But we found out we weren't so different after all, even if we're totally different on the outside."

Boss was looking mighty uncomfortable.

"What they're meaning to say is," said Big Boy, "even if we are afraid of you, you should still, um, come down to the jail, uh, for some Christmas supper?"

Truman saw something in Boss's eyes. Maybe it was a shred

of human decency, or maybe his eyes were misting up from their attempt at friendship—

"No," Boss said, breaking the spell.

"What?" said Truman.

Boss struggled for words. Truman could see the battle going on in his head. Finally, Boss threw his hands up and said, "All right, let's go."

"Where?" asked Nelle.

"My house."

38
Battle of Souls

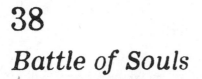

Mudtown had a quiet sadness to it on Christmas Day. There was nobody singing carols or building snowmen or playing with their Christmas toys. The white of the snow covered up the muck and mess but made the shantytown seem lonelier for it.

Bud had to park the truck at the edge of the neighborhood because the road was too narrow and slippery to drive on. Boss led the way through a maze of unnamed streets that were just spaces between makeshift buildings.

He stopped in front of his shack, which was made of tin siding, cardboard, damaged plywood, and a tarpaulin. For Boss, it was home.

Inside was dark except for a lone candle. His mother was wearing a big blanket wrapped around her as she knitted. Four smaller kids were huddled inside the blanket for warmth. Truman could see stale bread and some kind of watery soup on the table.

Boss's mother looked up suddenly, surprised to see him and the others behind him. "Peter, what are you doing here?" she asked. "You only been gone an hour or so. And why are they here —" She paused, looking pained. "You're not in trouble, are ya?"

His eyes grew dark. "Where's Catfish?" he asked quietly.

Her face grew somber. "I wouldn't know, and if I did, I wouldn't tell you." It was clear that she knew, but before Boss could say anything, she added, "Never you mind, you stay with your new friends here . . ."

He looked at her and his four siblings. "They invited me down to the jail for dinner," he said.

She stared at him for the longest time. "Now, why would you want to do that?" she asked. "Miss Sook said—"

Boss turned and walked out. His mother looked at Truman. "Please don't go . . ."

Truman turned to follow Boss. The others did the same.

They all piled back into the truck, Boss in the flatbed because he was so big. Bud started the engine but sat there, letting it idle.

Truman reached into his pocket, pulled out his little notebook. So much was happening, he needed to jot things down to free up his head again. He scribbled a few notes and observations.

Bud watched him. "I haven't seen you writing anything since you been here. Usually, you always got that notebook of yours out, writing one thing or the other."

"A lot's been happening," Truman said thoughtfully. "I've been storing up."

Bud smiled grimly and hit the gas.

"Writing about your new friend Boss?" asked Nelle.

Truman glanced at the hulking mass sitting behind them in the truck bed. "Just because he isn't beating me up doesn't make us friends."

"I wonder if he knows that . . ." she said.

"Maybe he's settin' us a trap," Big Boy added nervously. "I don't trust him for nothin'."

"*We* invited him," said Truman.

"That's what worries me," said Big Boy.

They drove in silence along the bumpy road. Boss must've been freezing, but never let on. Nothing seemed to faze him.

When they came up behind the jailhouse, the first thing they noticed was the sheriff's car parked in back.

"That's either a good sign or a bad sign," said Bud.

He drove around the front of the jail, and that was when everyone saw the crowd that had gathered. Nelle pressed her face to the car window, worried.

"Least they ain't dressed in white," said Big Boy.

Bud's truck came to a squealing stop and some of the men by the front door of the jail turned to stare them down. Nelle knew most of them—local men, farmers, hardscrabble. Even though it was Christmas, they couldn't help themselves.

The front door was open. Maybe even busted open.

"Wait here," Bud said as he got out of the truck.

He walked slowly up to the men, exchanged a few words with them, then went in. Truman recognized a few men from Catfish's crew. He turned to Boss, who was scanning the crowd. When one of the men spotted him, Boss slid off the truck. The truck shifted, rising a few inches. He took a step, then stopped and motioned for them to follow.

Big Boy had an I-ain't-going-in-there look on his face, but Truman and Nelle knew they couldn't sit idly by. They followed.

Of course, Big Boy didn't want to be left alone, so he reluctantly got out too. When Boss started moving toward the crowd, he parted the mob like the Red Sea and made way for the others to trail in his wake.

"There might be trouble," whispered Truman to Nelle.

"What do you mean, *might?*" she replied.

But the oddest thing happened when they entered the jail. They heard singing.

39
Soothing the Beast

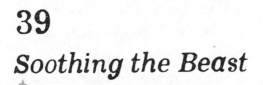

They say music soothes the savage beast. And it's a well-known fact that Christmas music, in particular, will melt anyone's heart. Men filled the lobby as they swarmed around the door leading into the back cell area. Nobody spoke because the singing drowned them out.

From the back room, Truman could hear Jenny, Sook, A.C., and several others, including the preacher and his choir, belting out "Angels We Have Heard on High." Their voices held a fierce determination to them, even if A.C. was way off-key. Bud had been corralled in, and when the singers saw Truman and the others, they were pulled in too.

It reminded Truman of the times he'd sneaked off to the black church and sung with the choir. There was an electricity in the air that made everything crackle. Even the Ezells, locked in their cell, seemed energized.

Boss stood towering above the rest. His daddy, Catfish, the former Grand Dragon, had some words to say to him, and they weren't nice ones. But Boss was bigger than his daddy now, and when he spotted that Christmas tree displayed in the corner, all decorated and lit up with bulbs, he was drawn to it like a moth to a flame.

He'd never had a tree like that.

When it came to singing "O Holy Night," a high voice unexpectedly took the lead: Boss. The others quieted down, and some of the choir stood with their mouths open and nothing coming out. There was something about the sight of an oversize bully like Boss Henderson singing with the voice of an angel. Even Truman was in awe.

Something inside Truman melted at that moment. Maybe it was the fear he'd always felt around Boss or the anger he felt at being afraid. But Boss's voice made all those feelings disappear. With that one song, Tru felt the weight of the curse finally being lifted.

You could see it in the men too. They'd come full of anger, a mob ready to do some damage. But Boss reminded them that it was Christmas. He made them think of their homes and their families and the shame of leaving them on this day to do something, well, un-Christmas-like. The men looked at one another with regret. Some wandered off back to their families, a few with grumbles of "This ain't over." Some watched with confusion and others looked on unaware that they were singing along under their breath.

The sheriff stood in the back, silent.

At the end of the song, nobody stood and cheered. Nobody felt they'd done anything except push off the inevitable for another day.

For the Ezells, another day was worth more than any Christmas present. It was a moment of bittersweet thankfulness they'd never forget. While the others stood around, Brown and Frank and his wife huddled in prayer.

The sheriff did one thing: He was able to get a promise from Catfish and his men that they'd let justice play out so as not to resort to other, cruder means. He convinced them that the guilty would get theirs soon, and that was good enough for them.

Catfish was a bit surprised when Sook asked him to stay and eat something. He eyed her suspiciously, but when he saw all the food and heard the grumbling in his stomach, he decided to stay.

Boss didn't say anything else to Truman that night, but he seemed content to eat Bama and Little Bit's feast. And afterward, Sook made Bud drive him and his daddy home, with the tree and all the leftovers they could carry.

40
The New Year

The morning after, the snow stopped and a grayness settled over the town like a cold blanket. Not cold enough to keep the snow on the ground for long, but enough to ensure there would be slush and mud everywhere for weeks to come.

Thanks to A.C., the rebuilding of Jenny's house began. He'd ignored her wishes and asked those who owed him for his services but hadn't been able to pay to come out and help. It was almost like an old-fashioned barn raising. The whole community turned out to do what they could: haul lumber, cut wood, hammer nails, or just feed the crew.

One day, the fire chief ambled over to Jenny as she was watching the workers' progress with A.C. smoking his pipe next to her. "Miss Jenny," he said, taking off his cap and wiping his sweaty brow like it was the middle of summer. "One of your neighbors came in and described what he believed to be the start of your fire."

Jenny and A.C. perked up. "Oh?" she said.

"Mr. Boular across the way told us that he saw lightning that night, but in reviewing his description, I'm fairly sure what he witnessed was an intense arcing from a downed electrical line, what we call a power flash."

A.C. studied him closely.

"I believe the power line snapped during the winds that night," the chief said, "sending a kind of fireball down the line and onto your roof."

"So . . . you mean it's not Mr. Lee's fault?" asked Jenny.

The fire chief laughed. "Not unless he's been playing God and can control Mother Nature!"

A.C. sat down on a pile of lumber to take it all in. Jenny placed her hand on his shoulder. "No, I do believe Mr. Lee is quite human, and a very decent one at that."

One burden was lifted from A. C. Lee's shoulders that day. But he still showed up every morning to help out when he could.

Truman wanted to spend as much time as he could with Nelle and Big Boy and Edison too. The three boys would wake up early and ride the two mules into town, or Nelle would hitch a ride out to the farm. Truman started writing again and Nelle brought over their old typewriter. Stories began to spark to life.

A.C. went back to work as part-time editor for the *Monroe Journal* and wrote editorials about the true meaning of Christmas. He wasn't being so subtle when he spoke about Joseph and Mary coming into Bethlehem as strangers and being rejected by everyone.

He asked Nelle and Truman if they wanted to write something from a kid's perspective, maybe about their friend Edison and the pool he'd told them he was digging. They thought it was a fine idea and took to being real reporters and not just pretend ones.

They interviewed Edison, and he told his side of things and why he was doing what he was doing. In the interest of fair play, they offered to interview Boss too, but he wasn't talking.

The next day, Edison told Truman that someone had shown up at night and dug out roughly half the pool, something that would have taken scrawny Edison weeks to do.

Had to be a big guy to pull that off.

A.C. said he would publish their piece on page six, the Sunshine Page, which was reserved for stories and poems by kids, usually funny adventures and whatnot. It was going to be for the New Year's Eve edition in a column he called "Wishes for the Future."

For that whole week, it felt like old times. Writing, telling stories, having adventures. Except not. They were older, practically teenagers now, and like the weather, real life was always there to interrupt whatever pretend world they played at.

When the New Year's Eve edition of the *Journal* came out, it seemed nobody wanted to read that kind of thing. Just as with A.C.'s articles, the town ignored the story and instead chose to talk about the effects the frost had had on their crops and when winter would end. They got on with life and waited for the new year to begin.

Before Truman could even think that maybe the curse had returned, Bud told him otherwise. "Never you mind them, Little Chappie. The public is a fickle group. You have been blessed by God's grace, that much is clear. I have always felt, Truman, that someday you will be famous. I know that I'll never live to see it, but I know it's true. You just keep telling your stories. The others will catch up to you."

Truman kept writing.

The county kept its promise of justice, or at least what passed for justice in the days of segregation, and on New Year's Eve, when people were raising a glass or kissing loved ones, Frank and Brown Ezell vanished from the jail and were never seen again. Nelle knew what had befallen them, but she did not speak of it to Truman or Big Boy. Instead, she lit a candle in her window and let it burn until there was no wax or wick left to see.

After New Year's had come and gone, Nelle began to wonder what Truman was going to do. For all the talk of the military school tracking him down for punishment, no one seemed to have followed him to Monroeville, least of all his mother. But

Nelle had noticed that he seemed to be spending more and more time at her house, even asking to stay the night there. Soon, she would find out why.

One day, Big Boy, Nelle, and Truman were hanging around the outer edges of the farm, helping Edison dig his pool. Well, *help* wasn't really the right word. Truman supervised and talked about how much they'd charge kids.

"Bet you could charge a quarter to swim here," said Truman.

"A qu-quarter?" said Edison. "Don't nobody got no qu-quarter round here."

"I have a quarter," said Truman, digging it out to show him.

"No n-normal kid," amended Edison. "I was thinking a n-nickel. Town p-pool charged a dime, and this h-half the size."

"Half?" said Nelle. "I bet you could fit twenty of these pools into that one. This is more like a pond."

While they were sitting around talking about admission prices, Big Boy noticed a car coming down the road.

A black Packard, a fancy car for these parts, slowly made its way along the muddy road, swerving around potholes and divots, heading for the farmhouse. Truman saw Big Boy staring and turned to see the automobile.

Truman was already the palest boy in the county, but he suddenly turned a shade whiter.

"Is that . . ." said Nelle.

Truman nodded. "Mother."

When the car grew close, the driver began honking, scaring the mules and the chickens and sending Queenie into a flurry of barking. The car pulled up to the house just as Jenny and Mary Ida came out onto the porch.

A man dressed in a fancy pinstriped suit emerged from behind the wheel, bearing flowers.

"Joe . . ." Truman said.

Joe popped around to the passenger side and opened the door, and out stepped Nina.

Truman took a breath but forgot to exhale. Nelle nudged him when he started to turn blue. "Breathe . . ."

He exhaled.

"Whatcha gonna do?" asked Big Boy.

Truman thought. "I could run away."

Nelle watched Nina and Joe talking with Jenny and Mary Ida. Nina was loud and overbearing, and Jenny didn't seem particularly pleased to see them.

"Where to?" asked Nelle.

"We could . . . we could . . ." said Truman.

"What do you mean, *we?* I got school next week," said Big Boy.

"And I got work to d-do," said Edison, looking at his pool.

Truman turned to Nelle. "We could hitch a ride . . . on a train. Jump the rails and head out to the great unknown. Maybe find the Mississippi and build a raft, just like Tom Sawyer and Huck Finn, and ride all the way to the Gulf. We could go to Mexico."

Nelle listened. It all seemed exciting.

"Or, better yet, I could write my old friend Satchmo—Louis Armstrong. He's a trumpet player in New Orleans. He could get me a job on one of those steamboats and I could tap-dance while he played, just like the old days. And you could go around collecting money from the patrons, and maybe you could develop your own act too—"

"I could teach golf!" said Nelle.

"You do *not* know how to play golf," said Big Boy.

"I caddy for my daddy when he plays, and he lets me swing on the driving range. He said I'm the best girl golfer in the county."

"You're the *only* girl golfer in the county, then," said Big Boy.

"I think that's a great idea. You could turn the upper deck into a driving range and try to hit the other rival boats—"

"Truman!"

The shout echoed across the muddy field. Truman and the others slunk down in the hole.

Jenny was calling and waving at him. "Truman! Come here!"

He ignored her and whispered in Nelle's ear, "We could live a life on the road, you and me, just like we always talked about. Going from town to town, living off the river or wherever a train would take us."

"That sounds swell, Truman," said Nelle.

"Truman!" Jenny was sounding more determined.

Nelle reached across and hugged him. "You should go."

Truman shook his head. "I'm not going back."

"Just tell them that. They'll understand," she said.

"She never understands. That's why she sent me to that horrible school in the first place," he said.

Jenny was standing on the porch with her hands on her hips. Nina was going inside with Mary Ida. But Joe turned and started walking toward them.

"He's coming over . . ." said Big Boy.

"It's now or never, Nelle. Won't you come with me?" Truman pleaded.

Nelle watched as Joe came closer. "I . . . I . . ."

"Truman, I see you," Joe called out from about fifty yards away.

Truman pulled on Nelle's sleeve. "We have to go. Now."

"I . . . I . . ."

"Truman, you son of a gun, are you playing hide-and-seek with your friends?" said Joe, trying not to get his fancy shoes too muddy. "Did you not hear Jenny calling?"

Nelle looked at Truman. "You can't keep running, Truman. You need to stand up for yourself. Tell them you are who you are and that there's no changing that."

Truman was crushed. "But . . . we'd have so much fun."

"You can come back and spend the summers here like you were supposed to," said Nelle. "And I promise I'll be better at writing. Maybe I can even come up to New York sometime . . ."

Truman stared at the ground; Nelle tried to reassure him. "You can do it," she said. "I promise I'll stay true to myself if you do too. Don't forget, *we* get to say what we make of our lives, not them. It's not all left to fate or curses, Truman. Don't change for anybody, not your mother or Joe—"

"Truman! Why don't you come when we call for you?" Joe said, towering over them in the hole. "You make me come out here and my shoes—" He frowned at the mud covering them. "Ugh. Come on, enough games. Your mother wants to talk to you. And then tomorrow, we go home."

Truman stared at Joe's shoes.

"Come on, Pinocchio. It's time—"

"I'm not going back," said Truman.

Joe frowned. "Truman . . ."

"Joe, you don't know what it was like in that military school! It was, it was—" Truman ran out of words.

Joe chuckled. "Oh, that . . ." He took out a big Cuban cigar and bit off the tip. "No, don't worry, you are not going back there." He lit the cigar and puffed on it, creating a cloud of white smoke all around him.

"What?" said Truman.

Joe waved his arm. "Bah, I told her it would never work. He's a—he's a special one, that Truman, I said. He'll never be like me!" He pounded his chest like Tarzan, then softened.

"I'm not going to change, Joe. If she won't accept me, I'll run away again."

Joe nodded at Truman, impressed. "I believe it. I wish I could fly, but I can't. Your mother wants to be a star—but who's kidding who, yes? She wants you to be more—to be more manly, like a real boy. But I say he's not like the real Pinocchio. There's no magic fairy in military school . . ." He rolled his eyes.

Truman sighed. "Then what?"

Joe puffed, thinking. "We're moving up to Connecticut. Nice neighborhood. Private schools. Joe pays for a good school for our Truman. No uniforms. No military." He looked back at the house, but everyone had gone in.

He knelt down to be closer to Truman's face. "They even have a writing program, you know. School paper and all that. It will be better, trust Joe. I'm not gonna lie to you."

"I don't know," said Big Boy. "Sounds okay to me . . ."

Nelle squeezed his hand. "Truman, do it," she said. "It'll be okay."

Joe turned to Nelle for the first time. "You must be Nellie. We didn't meet formally last time. But I know you—you're the girl who thinks she's a boy."

"Nelle. Her name is Nelle," said Truman. "And she can be however she wants to be."

Joe held up his hands and smiled. "I didn't mean nothing by it. Any friend of Truman's is a friend of mine." He put out his hand.

Nelle stared at it suspiciously but then slowly shook it.

Joe looked at the others. "Big Boy, right? You don't look so big . . ."

Big Boy shook his head. "Only when I was a baby," he said, glancing at Truman.

Joe turned to Edison. "You," he finally said. "You almost as dark as me!" he said with a laugh. Edison was confused because he was way darker than Joe. "What're you doing? Digging a hole to China?"

"Maybe we are," said Truman. "You tell Lillie Mae or Nina or whatever she wants to call herself that I'm busy at the moment. Tell her I'll come back home with you. But when I'm ready."

Joe straightened up, puffing his cigar. "You know the secret to a good cigar?"

Truman shrugged.

"You can't force the leaves," Joe said. "They are ready when they are ready. Some grow fast, some grow big. But usually, the more delicate ones have a bolder taste."

He took a good strong pull and let the smoke drift from his lips. "Me? I prefer a bold cigar," he said as he walked back to the house.

Nineteen Years Later
Christmas Morning, 1956

Epilogue

The snow fell in a flurry, cascading down through the skyscrapers that blotted out the dreary morning sky over New York. It had been almost eight years since Nelle had moved to Manhattan to become a writer. That was the year that thousands of ex-GIs still lived in huts dotting the shores of Brooklyn and Staten Island. It was also the year Truman's first novel came out, turning him into something of a literary sensation at age twenty-three. To Nelle, now thirty and worn down by her job as an airline reservation assistant, writing seemed more like a distant hobby.

She tightened her scarf and pulled her overcoat close. It was freezing, and she liked it that way. She put on her glasses to see the address on the upscale apartment building to which she was headed.

"Well, if it isn't the Jane Austen of the South!"

Nelle would have known that voice anywhere. She turned and saw Truman, dressed in a fine camelhair overcoat, a floppy hat, and a scarf that reached to the ground.

"Well, if it isn't the precocious, self-confident, and gifted Mr. Capote—"

He grinned. "*Genuinely* gifted, I think they said."

Nelle hugged him. "The *New York Times* does tend to exaggerate, don't they?"

Smile, smile; kiss, kiss.

Truman looked her up and down and *tsked*. "You've been here all this time and still you look like you just escaped from a Southern penal colony. I simply have to take you shopping. Maybe I'll get you something from Tiffany's. That'll be my gift to you."

She shook her head and laughed. "Truman, just accept the fact that I'll never be like you. I don't wear jewelry and I can do my own shopping, thanks."

He glanced at his manicured fingernails. "Suit yourself. Just be glad I didn't bring you a fruitcake for Christmas!"

They laughed and she hugged her purse, which contained not one but two fruitcakes. They made their way into the lobby, where the doorman was expecting them. "I know the way," said Nelle even before the man could explain.

Truman winked at him. "Merry Christmas. That's for you, darling." He handed the man a twenty-dollar bill.

On the elevator up, Nelle said, "You shouldn't throw your money around like that. Just because you're famous doesn't mean you're rich."

"*Yet,*" said Truman. "But we can pretend. How come you didn't go home for Christmas? You can't leave Big Boy all alone down there."

"Big Boy is doing just fine flying his ol' crop-duster. As for me, the airlines only gave me Christmas Day off this year. It's their busy time, you know."

"Oh yes, the airline business. Must be tough making reservations for people flying all over the world while you're stuck here." He smiled and hugged her arm. "I'm glad. I don't see enough of you."

She always felt odd hanging out with Tru's circle of New York friends. She was still seen as an outsider, a country bumpkin. "Truth be told, I miss Christmas at home," she said. "The sound of hunting boots, the chilly night air smelling of pine needles—"

"Your father trying to sing 'Angels We Have Heard on High' in tune . . ."

Nelle smiled wistfully. "I'm glad you're here. You're the only one around who knows . . ."

The elevator pinged and the doors opened. Across the hall was the apartment of Michael and Joy Brown, Truman's oldest New York friends, who had taken Nelle under their wing when

Truman had to leave town the summer she'd first moved there. Through the open door, Nelle and Tru could see the warm glow of the fireplace and smell the enchanting scent of bacon, pancakes, and freshly brewed coffee.

"This must be heaven," said Nelle.

Out stepped Joy and Michael in their matching robes and pajamas. "There they are, our two writers!" said Joy.

"One," said Nelle. "I'm just the apprentice."

"Oh, look at how modest she's become," said Truman. "You have real talent, Nelle. You just need to apply yourself. Your time will come."

Later, they sat around the Christmas tree, their bellies full and satisfied. It was time to open presents, and knowing Nelle couldn't afford anything expensive, they'd suggested bargain-basement gifts. Nelle handed out her modest but thoughtful gifts of used books, which had cost her a grand total of $4.60 from a nearby thrift store. Truman was never one to be modest; his gifts consisted of glass paperweights with delicate flowers inside. "I found them at an estate sale. They were a bargain, I swear!"

Michael and Joy exchanged gifts of lovely scarfs and knickknacks but neglected to give one to Nelle. She was too polite to say anything.

After a dramatic pause, Joy smiled and said slyly, "Oh, I think there's something over there for you, Nelle." She pointed at the tree.

Epilogue

Nelle stood up and saw, hidden in its branches, a small envelope with her name written on it. She blushed, for some reason.

"Well, go on, open it!" said Truman.

She opened the flap and took out a simple note card on which was handwritten:

You have one year off from your job to write whatever you please. Merry Christmas.

Nelle didn't know what to make of it. She read it aloud. "What . . . does this mean?"

"It means what it says," said Michael.

She didn't know how to respond. "You can't do this. It's such a great gamble. You shouldn't risk your money like that."

Joy smiled. "It's no risk, honey. You're a sure thing."

Nelle's eyes grew moist.

"You can finally write a novel, like you've always wanted to," said Truman. "What do you think you'll you write about, Nelle?"

Nelle was stunned. "I'm . . . not sure."

Truman stood up and put his arm around her as she stared at the note. "Write about what you know," he said.

And right then, she looked at Truman and knew instantly that she would write about Alabama. About growing up with

Tru and Big Boy, about her father and his trial, about Sonny and Boss, about drinking sweet tea on the porch and all the goings-on in Monroeville.

She would write about home.

The End

Author's Note

Like its predecessor, *Tru & Nelle,* this fictional tale is loosely inspired by the childhood friendship of two of the greatest American writers of the twentieth century, Truman Capote and Nelle Harper Lee. They grew up as next-door neighbors in the tiny remote town of Monroeville, Alabama, along with Truman's cousin Big Boy.

While the basic construct of the stories are fiction, all the characters and places in this book are based on real people and the town of Monroeville in the 1930s. Many of the events were taken from things that actually happened. For instance, when he was nine, Truman did move to New York to live with his mother, who'd changed her name to Nina. A couple of years later, there was a custody hearing during which Arch Persons tried to destroy Nina's reputation in order to send the boy back to Jenny's. Nina won but not too long after ended up sending Truman to St. John's Military Academy outside New York City, hoping to turn him into a real boy. Truman did run away several times as a youth (once with another girl, to make Nelle jealous). Jenny's house did burn to the ground on a frozen night when A.C. Lee overloaded his fireplace to keep warm. Truman did drive a car as a preteen, scaring his passengers out of their wits. Jenny's cook was a voodoo priestess. A man like Indian Joe did make whiskey for Sook's fruitcakes. A mule did grab one of the kids' heads in its mouth (though it was Nelle's). Tru and Sook did ride the aspen trees that surrounded Big Boy's farm.

Boss is inspired by one of Truman's childhood bullies, whom he and Big Boy once knocked out (in self-defense) and thought they'd killed. This resulted in Sook's inviting the bully over for dinner to make amends, as Truman captured in his story "The Thanksgiving Visitor."

The Klan is and was real; the Deep South in the 1930s was rooted in segregation and unjust Jim Crow laws. Black folks had to stand to the side when whites passed, regardless of their age. The tale of the mail carrier who encounters the Klan is true, but it happened to Lillie Mae and Mary Ida's father, Popper. The trial of the Ezells was the first and last criminal case A.C. Lee ever took on, but it occurred earlier in his career. His loss and the loss of his clients' lives scarred him forever. It became the basis for the trial at the center of *To Kill a Mockingbird* (which was written only after Michael and Joy Brown gave Nelle that astonishing Christmas gift in New York). Truman went on to write several wonderful Christmas tales in his lifetime, including a classic story about Sook called "A Christmas Memory."

The rest is make-believe and hearsay peppered with real incidents plucked out of time and put in a different order, perhaps with different players—speculative fiction in search of poetic truths.

Acknowledgments

I would like to thank my editor, Julia Richardson, for going along with me on this ride, even though the concept kept changing. Thanks for being flexible and thinking it was closer to brilliant than crazy. Thanks to the team of fine folks over at Houghton Mifflin Harcourt (Lisa DiSarro, Amanda Acevedo, Tara Sonin, Ruth Homberg, Whitney Leader-Picone, and Mary Wilcox), plus Tracy Roe for her copy edits, Colleen Fellingham for her proofreading, and Sarah Watts for her wonderful covers.

Thanks to all the teachers, librarians, booksellers, and readers who loved the first book. Especially all the adults who took a flyer on reading a book for kids just because they loved Truman or Harper Lee so much.

As always, thanks to my agent, Edward Necarsulmer IV, for thinking a *Tru & Nelle* sequel covering three different time periods was a pretty cool idea.

Thanks to the town of Monroeville for welcoming this obvious outsider. To Alisha Linam and Alabama Center for Literary Arts for inviting me to speak in the actual Monroe County Courthouse where A.C. represented clients. To the fantastic Monroe County Courthouse Museum, especially Nathan

Carter, grandson of Mary Ida, and Wanda Green for allowing us full access to the courthouse and its contents, and George Jones for keeping the stories of his hometown alive. Thanks also to the good people at the Ol' Curiosities and Book Shoppe in Monroeville for hosting me.

Thanks to Charles J. Shields for his fantastic bio of Harper Lee, *Mockingbird,* and for encouraging me to do book two; to e. E. Charlton-Trujillo for suggesting we make a film about my trip to Monroeville and then doing it (amazingly!); and to Jim Bailey for editing said film to perfection (you can see it on my website). Thanks to the Truman Capote Papers at the New York Public Library Archives and the Truman Capote Estate for their assistance.

Thanks to all the writers who've written or edited books about Truman Capote and Harper Lee, among them: Gerald Clarke, George Plimpton, M. Thomas Inge, Lawrence Grobel, Kerry Madden-Lunsford, and especially Marianne M. Moates, who captured Big Boy's childhood adventures in a way that gave me the voice and spirit of their young lives, and Truman's aunt Tiny, aka Marie Rudisill, whose many writings have captured the time and place with a spectacular dose of Southern embellishment.

As always, special thanks to my family for all their support. None of this would happen without them.

A very special thanks to Truman Capote and Nelle Harper Lee for being true to themselves and inspiring these stories.

G. Neri speaks at the Monroe County Courthouse, where A. C. Lee
defended cases as Nelle and Tru watched from the balcony.

Sook's Pecan Fruitcake

Sook didn't start making fruitcakes until she was fifty, but then she did so religiously every Christmas till she passed away. In her mind, for Southerners, fruitcake was almost a birthright. She and Truman hauled the cakes around town in a wicker doll carriage to hand them out as gifts. She even sent one to the president every year. She kept them sealed in red tin containers; when you pried off the lid, you almost fell over from the fumes.

Never had a fruitcake before? Well, now you can—all you have to do is make one from Sook's updated recipe below. Remember, like a fine wine, the longer it sits, the better it tastes!

- ⅔ cup butter
- ¾ cup brown or white sugar
- Pinch of salt
- 3 eggs
- 2 cups sifted all-purpose flour
- 1 teaspoon baking powder
- ½ teaspoon each ground nutmeg and allspice
- 1 teaspoon ground cinnamon

Sook's Pecan Fruitcake

- ¾ cup kumquats softened in boiling water, drained, and peeled, then cut into small pieces (or use dried apricots, if need be)
- 1 cup chopped pecans
- ¾ cup golden raisins
- ½ cup chopped candied pineapple
- 2 tablespoons applesauce
- 3 tablespoons milk or apple juice
- Grated rind of 1 lemon
- Grated rind of 1 orange

Preheat oven to 325 degrees. Grease a large loaf pan with butter.

In a bowl, whip butter with sugar and salt, beating the mixture until it is smooth. Add eggs. Stir in flour sifted with baking powder and spices. Add the remaining ingredients. Stir.

Pour the batter into the prepared pan and bake for 1 hour. Remove the cake from the pan. Eat warm or at room temperature, with jam.

Merry Christmas!